D1500186

THE
DESCENT

Gina Berriault

Benedictine University Library
Mesa Campus
225 E. Main Street
Mesa, AZ 85201

NORTH POINT PRESS *San Francisco* 1986

Copyright © 1960, 1986 by Gina Berriault
Printed in the United States of America
Library of Congress Catalogue Card Number: 85-72986
ISBN: 0-86547-220-3

Cover illustration: *Disasters of War*, plate 71,
"Against the Common Good," by Francisco Goya y Lucientes.
Etching, aquatint, and drypoint, 150 × 190 mm.
Courtesy of The Fine Arts Museums
of San Francisco
Cover design: David Bullen

North Point Press
850 Talbot Avenue
Berkeley, California
94706

Indeed I live in the dark ages!
A guileless word is an absurdity.
A smooth forehead betokens
A hard heart. He who laughs
Has not yet heard the terrible tidings.

BERTOLT BRECHT: *To Posterity*

The Descent

1

Upon their arrival at the airport of the nation's capital, Arnold T. Elkins and family were greeted by a young man who introduced himself as Radovan Wells, appointed to serve as Elkins' aide. A tall and thin young man with a crew cut and a brown silk suit, he smiled upon them as embracingly as if they were his own family, himself their progenitor, and shook hands all around, with Arnold, with Alma, his wife, and with the two adolescent daughters who each held out a white-gloved hand, the younger resolutely, the older tremulously, her purse, which dangled by its strings from her wrist, hanging open like a mouth. A crowd of men, women, and children was gathered around an old dust-gray car in the parking lot, and toward this waiting scene he led them. Several men with famous faces were in the forefront, congressmen and senators of the political party of the President, and these were introduced to the family, their welcoming words and handshakes recorded for the press by men with cameras and with notepads. A small girl in a faded but fresh cotton dress and cheap, whitened shoes, her hair cut somewhat unevenly, timidly presented to Arnold a bouquet of nasturtiums and daisies. The young man then swung open the car door, and when the family was settled inside, he folded his long legs under the steering wheel, slammed the door with an unlocked sound, and drove away, explaining, as the family was waving back to the crowd, that his choice of a car so obviously modest was of a significance that he would explain later, when they reached the apartment he had already rented for them.

The neighborhood they found themselves in was one of dingy apartment houses with dead curtains at the windows. The young man braked the car before a narrow yellow-brick building, on whose sidewalk the photographers from the airport were already gathered, snapping pictures of the residence. "Now don't be alarmed. This isn't as nice as some, but it's clean and it's got tradition," Radovan told the family as they waited within the bile-green tiled entranceway for a response to his long finger's pressing the button over the manager's card.

The knob on the glass door, which bore in dim gold letters the name LINCOLN APTS., buzzed loudly, and the young man, giving the knob a deft, merciless twist, led them in over a carpet, in a circle-and-triangle pattern, laid down in the 1920's. They were met by an elderly woman with sulphur-blond hair who emerged from the far end of a narrow dark hallway. She was expecting them: her dress was party style and her heels were high and her hand trembled with the honor of clasping the hands of a Presidential cabinet member and his family. With a youthfulness in her frail white legs, she led them up the carpeted stairs that smelled faintly of cat urine, their way lit by dim globes burning in niches behind rippled amber glass. They were followed by the newsmen, stamping and stumbling, their voices echoing dampishly down the hallways.

Up in the apartment of large and faded rooms, the landlady gone, the curious tenants gone, the newsmen gone (after posing the family among the lumps and hollows of the sofa's coral upholstery), and the door closed, Radovan, bending his long leg over a corner of the dining table and pushing aside a red glass vase holding stalks of festive gladioli, informed them that the post of Secretary for Humanity was to be an austerity post. "They figured," he said, "that the Early Christian type would be best. Nothing showy, no suites, no fur coats for the wife." Lean as he was, the young man appeared to be well-fed, and the definition he was giving was not comprehended by his own eyes. "The title," he said, tapping his chest, "will come from the heart."

Arnold, having expected no material gain from the post, found no fault with the program. The honor of his appointment was, to him, so great that his only wish was to prove by his deeds in office that he had been a happy choice. But he saw the young man glancing uneasily at his wife and daughters, who were sitting erect on the sofa's edge, their hats and gloves still on; he saw the young man wondering if this reluctance to relax and to make themselves at home implied an opposition to being deprived of that which they had hoped to gain. The prospect of austerity was not troubling to them, Arnold knew; each of them was troubled by her own particular need.

So impressed was his wife by the magnitude of the post that she doubted his capacity to fill it, and with furrowed brow she absorbed the young man's instructions in the hope of remembering whatever her husband might forget. Bernice, his sixteen-year-old daughter, was in the habit of envisioning perils, and her father's acceptance of the post placed the family in the greatest peril ever, for the town they had come from seemed a less likely bomb target than the city they were now in. The tips of her ears morbidly alert through her pale hair that fell straight to her collar, she listened to the young man's every word, resembling a medieval prisoner sentenced to the rack. Rebecca, the younger, had devoted the thirteen years of her life to becoming as unlike her sister as possible; physically, the job was done for her already, for she resembled her mother, black-haired, athletic, and animated, but this was not enough, and so strenuously did she now try to convey her dedication to her father's task that a feverish gaze resulted, one the young man might be misinterpreting as a sign of hysteria rushing in to fill the void left by his call for austerity.

"I'm certain that we shall be happy here," Arnold assured the young man. "In fact, we'd be uncomfortable in more comfortable surroundings."

Radovan slid farther back onto the table until only the tip of one smart shoe touched the threadbare rug. "It pleased me so much when I learned of my appointment as your assistant," he said, "because this post of yours is a tremendous idea. You remember how the President outlined it in his letter to you? So clear a call that a man would run out barefoot to answer it: 'You will devote yourself to the task of preserving the peace, assuring humanity that the first missile may never be fired, that the bombs may never fall, and that in the not distant future all nations will sit down together and partake of the wondrous fruits that this Nuclear Age has yet to offer.' " With the sudden kindliness that one directs toward a child who has been neglected in an adult conversation, he said to Alma, "My great-grandmother had an aphorism embroidered in a frame, reading, 'Patience is a tree whose roots are bitter but whose fruit is sweet.' It's an appropriate thing to quote if you're interviewed, don't you think?"

"The title seems a bit topheavy to me," Arnold said, massaging his brow. "Humanity covers a lot of territory, you know."

Radovan nodded eagerly. "That's right, it does. And this post will serve *all* humanity. When you strive for us, you're striving for aspiring humanity everywhere."

Arnold rubbed his knee reflectively. "There's another question," he said. "Why am I the right man for the job? The letter from the President simply noted that I possessed many attributes, and the fellow who interviewed me discussed with me the world crisis and that was about all; and when I asked him what the attributes were he replied that I was a modest man if I was unaware of them. So I would appreciate your telling me why I was chosen, if you know."

At this, Radovan permitted an essential boyishness to spread through his body. He left his perch to sink down next to Bernice on the sofa and, after lighting cigarettes for himself and Arnold with a tiny, flat, gold lighter, he leaned forward, smacking his hands together. The formalities were over, his manner implied, and they could get down to sowing the seeds of a friendship that ought to be springing up between himself and this family. "It's like this," he began. "They wanted a man who enjoyed some prestige. Not anybody in business, because to some people that connotes a self-centeredness. So they figured the best place to look was among the professions, and since medicine and law are often lucrative, they narrowed it down to scholars. Among the scholars, the best man, they figured, was one whose field was mankind. Well, philosophy sounded too highbrow—it does to the average man, that is —and anthropology is too much concerned with the primitive and the past, sociology sounded statistical and cold, and so history won out. Then they decided that he must be a modest fellow, somebody with some accomplishments but not too many; not a four-star professor, they're intimidating, but almost one, maybe somebody who just didn't make the grade or hadn't made it yet, like a lot of us—an associate professor. It simmers down to this: You're someone the average man can identify with and someone he can look up to, and you're someone who's interested in *him*, the average man. That answer your question?"

"But why," asked Arnold, "was I chosen from among so many associate professors of history in the country?"

Radovan picked at the furled edge of his ear, an activity that established an intimacy between himself and the family. "The fellow who was sent out to sound your depths, he did more than just interview *you*, you know. He interviewed a lot of other people around DeVelbiss, Iowa, around Langshank County. He discovered that your grandfather was a farmer, a man remembered for his longevity and his honesty and his haranguing around on every issue put to the vote, nothing too small or too big to corner his neighbor about, a roots-in-the-earth sort of man, and that your father was quite a figure, too. A lawyer, a small-town lawyer who was known all over the state, sort of a popular hero who took a case into court without fee if he thought the cause was just and knew the client was penniless. You can't top that kind of a background when you're looking for a man to fill the kind of post yours is." In the young man's glancing blue eyes was a sense of accomplishment; he seemed to have won a prize for himself, as he had promised somebody he would. "When he asked around about *you*, yourself, when he asked around among your colleagues and your students what they thought about you, he found that you were quite a favorite. No enemies, no word spoken against you. Everybody liked your way of poking fun at history's great figures, at customs and practices, things like that. They said you could get incensed over an injustice done to somebody a hundred years ago, but that you never got thrown off balance by temporal issues, by today's issues. That is, you weren't afraid to criticize today's heroes, but you weren't the kind to go overboard on a hate campaign. They liked you for that combination of detachment from the present and passionate curiosity about the past. Anyway, the man came back and said they all liked you." And guessing how much it must please the wife and daughters to hear of the high respect accorded the man of the family by the citizens of DeVelbiss, he smiled at them in their row of three on the sofa.

Arnold shifted in his chair, throwing his arm over the back of it in an attempt to escape this praise which was the sum of confidential interviews. He remembered that morning, six weeks ago, when the letter from the President had been delivered to him, the letter informing him of the creation of the post and requesting him to consent to an interview by a member of the President's staff. It was early in the summer; he had been at work upon the third part of his "Cultural History of Iowa" for the *DeVelbiss College Quarterly*, and his wife and daughters were playing tennis over at the college courts, and in the empty house, in the house to himself, he had read and reread the letter, sunk down in the leather chair in the living room. How it had pleased him to learn that the President and his advisers regarded him as more worthy than he, himself, had ever realized, yet how it had also pleased him to think that, at last, he was to come into his own, that Alma's designation of him as one of the most humane of human beings was now to be verified by an award. After that moment of confusion, he had perceived himself for what he was, he had defined himself simply: a humble man and a proud man, a critical yet compassionate man, a man of faults and virtues—and he had judged himself acceptable for the post. That balance could not long endure, and in the weeks that followed, while he studied transcripts of summit meetings, of foreign ministers' meetings, a day of self-doubting, like a day of fitful winds banging at the windows, would be followed by a day of near exultation, a day of unbearable impatience to prove his capacity for the job. Arrived at last in the nation's capital, folded now into this huge thumped-out chair that smelled of cabbage and stale tobacco, he was again beset by doubts, and all the praise from his neighbors and all the accomplishments (his own and his father's and his grandfather's) seemed not enough to qualify a man for the task of untying—or helping to untie—that knot of the world's tension. He had asked his questions and got his answers, but something was lacking, and since he could not name the lack he located it within himself.

"Their choosing a history teacher," Alma was saying, "I'm surprised that it was a last choice, that they narrowed it down, as you said. We thought, back home when we got the letter, that it was the first choice. After Sputnik, you know, this country began to respect its scientists more, they were elevated, and everybody's son and nephew is studying to be a scientist now. But we thought, when we got the letter, that the time had come for elevating another kind of scholar, men who'd be consulted by the government and maybe even be appointed to office, men who'd devote their time to figuring out how . . ."

Radovan's vigorous smiling interrupted her. "Do you know what came first?" he asked her, encouraged by her stirring to life. "They wanted a family man, and *that* came first. The fellow reported that the Elkins family was happy and harmonious, and attractive in an unstartling way. The fact that you are a piano teacher was of great influence, too. So many children take piano lessons, you know, and they and their mothers will look up to you, an archetypal piano teacher. They'll feel neighborly. Arnold," he said, using the given name for the first time, "will be closely allied with his family in this post. The family will accompany him on his missions and strengthen his symbolic value. Somebody the Family of Man can get close to." Standing up with a swiftness that implied he had been sitting too long in the company of charming women, he said to Arnold, "Shall we go now? You've an appointment with the Secretary of Defense, Jim Eversledge." And to Alma, "This time it's just him."

Alma and the girls trailed after the men to the door, where Bernice, nervously flipping back a long tendril of hair that was curling at her throat, addressed herself to Radovan, in a voice unnaturally high with respect for him. "What do you think of the possibility of war by accident?" she asked, striving to phrase her question formally and thus conceal her personal involvement in it.

Radovan, transfixed by her adjuring gaze, was unable, for several seconds, to answer. "I suppose there's always that possibility," he said, clearing his throat at the same time he spoke.

"Do you think there'll be a war by accident anyway?" she asked, framing her question differently in order to ask it twice.

"Anyway?" he inquired.

"I mean *anyway*, in spite of what you said that the first missile would probably never be fired. Could there be a war by accident, anyway?"

Becky stared down at her shoes, embarrassed by her sister's attempt to force a clairvoyant answer from him. "She saw a movie about an H-bomb war by accident and she's been worried ever since," she explained. "That was three years ago, and she gets more worried with each year because somebody in the movie was saying how the possibility of war by accident increases year by year. He was saying that a radar man might mistake a meteor for a missile or he might go crazy from watching the skies. Right after that the accident happened." She bent down to scratch her ankle. "I worry about something more basic," she said, turning her head to look up at him sideways.

"More basic?" Radovan asked.

"Like the question of how we got into that bind." She gazed up at him, still sideways, waiting for an answer whose wisdom would match her own, though hers was a paraphrasing of her father's answer to Bernice and to anybody, back in DeVelbiss, who voiced the same fear.

"You girls ought to meet the James Eversledge kids," Radovan said. "They know everything about everything on an Atlas, a Jupiter, an Honest John—every missile in the arsenal. Perhaps we can arrange an afternoon get-together, here or at the Eversledges'. Kids are so knowledgeable these days," he said to Arnold, putting his hand on Arnold's arm to remind him that the door was open and that he should proceed down the hallway. "No subject is foreign to them."

So eager was Arnold to assume his duties at once that not until Radovan had juggled the car into traffic did he begin to think it odd that his first conference in the capital should be with James Eversledge.

"Why Eversledge?" he asked.

"He wants to brief you," Radovan explained.

"What's Eversledge got to do with me?" Arnold insisted. "He's got his own Defense Department to worry about."

"To put it in the vernacular, he's your boss," Radovan informed him, glancing out at a group of sidewalk spectators watching a yellow pile driver at work, shoring up the sides of an excavation for a mass fallout shelter. The blows of the pile driver reverberated in the car. "You're not a full-fledged member of the cabinet, you know. You're a quasi-member, as it was explained to you in the letter. Oh, you're under the President, you're in the executive, but you'll be conferring with Eversledge. There's no cause for complaint. After all, the Defense Secretary is now second in command. He and the President"—and he held up two fingers—"are like this, and have been ever since Congress passed the recommendations of the Eversledge Inquiry. The Inquiry came out in '59 and became a law the same year, there was no denying the logic of it. And when Harmon Harringer was elected in '60, he chose Eversledge for his Defense Secretary, shook him loose from Redi-Sledge Aircraft. The best man for the job, Harmon said, was the man who saw and suggested the new dimensions of it. So," he said, glancing restlessly far ahead as if tiring of Arnold's questing company, "you're right up there."

Arnold, closing his eyes for a moment against the loss of equilibrium resulting from the day's incessant travel by plane and by auto, was confronted by the image of his companion as someone he had seen before, long ago. Was it in a troubling dream, years ago when he was a novice teacher? He was strolling the campus and at his side was a student with a respectful voice that didn't match up with the face that insinuated a knowledge beyond the teacher's, and, parting company after conversing together on a high, gratifying level, the student put out his foot and tripped the teacher. The car swung Arnold against Radovan as the latter brought it to a sudden stop before classical steps, shallow, white, and half a block long.

"Some day," said Radovan, as they shot upward in an elevator of the Triangle, headquarters of the Defense Department, "I'll show you around the building. It's triangular, you know, for symbolic reasons. It represents a missile pointing east."

Arnold was escorted through the anteroom, furnished with one oak waiting bench of a kind he had not seen since his childhood and then in the school principal's office; through an aide's office, equipped with a scratched, gray metal filing cabinet and a simple office desk; and into his own office, and there, while Radovan picked up the phone and informed Eversledge's office that Elkins had arrived, Arnold glanced around at the bareness broken only by his heavy oak desk and a few visitors' chairs, two of which were straight-backed library chairs and one of leather, its seat contoured into a hard saddle by years of use. The shabby collection seemed incongruous within the walls of the room, the exterior wall of glass and the rest of black-and-white plastic combined with walnut paneling. "Someone," he said, when his aide had completed the call, "must have gone to a lot of trouble collecting the oddments here."

Radovan put his hands into his pockets and hunched his shoulders appealingly. "Not much trouble," he said.

"Do you suppose," Arnold ventured, "that you might be going too far? I myself am in accord with Buddha who, in his deer-park sermon, after years of crawling on his belly, skin and bones and covered with vermin, concluded that there was not much to be gained in carrying things to extremes."

Radovan frowned with delicate puzzlement. "But you said something about being uncomfortable in more comfortable surroundings."

"I'm not complaining for myself," Arnold hastened to explain. "I am only wondering if I might appear more odd than virtuous."

The young man gazed down at his shoes to muse upon an answer, and finding, perhaps, that their elegance gave away his own belief that virtue is rewarded by success and its signs, he gazed up, instead, at the ceiling, but was confronted by a large, luminous sphere of fluted white plastic, a modern light fixture that someone had neglected to take down. "The essential appeal of a Secretary for Humanity is this: someone uninterested in himself, almost unaware of himself. Someone interested, instead, in everybody else. It's a difficult assignment," he said, "even for the wisest of men."

After one brief knock, a man whom Arnold recognized as James Eversledge entered the room as Radovan leaped to fling the door wider. A most physically fit fellow of forty, Arnold's own age, with ripples of black hair beginning high above his long, handsome face, he advanced with the buoyancy of a candidate breasting his way through a crowd of constituents and extended his hand to Arnold.

They sat down together, Arnold in the swivel chair, Eversledge in a visitor's chair, and Radovan on a corner of the desk. "I don't like to summon a new man to my office," Eversledge said. "Makes him feel that I'm handing down orders from my sanctum sanctorum. This way, my coming by makes a man feel creative in his own right, and that's what we want. We can be grim around here, too. We've got the free world to protect and we're grim about it. Each man respects the men above him for their experience and their acuity and their devotion. But we believe that each man should be made to feel his own worth, also." Crossing his legs and laying his hand upon his top knee, a position a guest affects to put the host at ease, he said warmly, "Welcome to the Defense Department."

Arnold, taken by the potency of this democratic procedure, asked at once, "Why the Defense Department?"

"That bothered him all the way over," Radovan said.

"Where else? Where would *you* put yourself?" Eversledge asked.

"The State Department, perhaps?" Arnold suggested.

"Not now, not after the Inquiry," Eversledge replied. "If you understood the theory behind the legislation granting increased influence to the Secretary of Defense, you wouldn't figure, as you do now, that you're a square peg in a round hole. The defense of the nation is the nation's biggest task. We've got a sixty-billion-dollar appropriation this year, not counting the shelter program, and Mr. Taxpayer wants the best defense for his money. We're organized to give him the best. No longer is the Defense Secretary only an arbitrator of disputes among the services —the Air Force, the Army, the Navy. The Chiefs of Staff don't dispute any more. In the first place, they've got, at last, a wide-lens view that minimizes service boundaries, and in the second place, they've got a chairman who's my top military adviser, and they bring their troubles and their ideas to him. That leaves the Secretary of Defense free to mold high military policy, free to mold the defense of the nation. We now develop weapons with a rapidity my predecessors could only dream about, and this organizational ascendancy, this efficiency, we've got is a result, let me repeat, of the Inquiry."

"It appears to me that we're further apart than I thought we were when I asked my question," Arnold said. "We're poles apart. You're in office to see that we build more weapons and I'm in office to try to render them null and void."

Eversledge's wafting hand called for patience and a little thought. "You say that you belong in the State Department. Let me tell you, then, that our Secretary of State, Calvert Witting, confers with us before leaving on a mission. He learns what's in production, what's on the drawing board, even what's on the minds of our research corps. I've often told him he ought to move into the Triangle with us. What I want to impress you with is this: When our delegates sit down at a conference, at any conference at any level, they're only as effective as their country is strong, military-wise. We put it this way: Military capability is the launching pad of diplomacy."

Arnold shifted in his chair, thoughtfully. "I can see," he said, "that the problem of disarmament is not a simple one. Our delegates must consider, first and foremost, what *not* to give up, and no doubt the delegates from the Soviet Union are also charged to observe the maxim you quoted, or a similar one of their own."

The Secretary of Defense massaged his eyelids with the tips of his fingers, his hands rotating in a patient rhythm above his snow-white shirt cuffs set with square topaz links. "That's putting it rather too simply," he said. "That implies an unwillingness on our part to consider a proposal on its merits. Let me explain it another way," he said, opening his eyes to gaze at Arnold. "You must remember that for the Russians a disarmament conference is *not* that. They think of a conference as an opportunity to weaken us. We therefore hold to our spectrum of weapons, hold to our freedom to experiment with them, and hold to our right to develop any new weapons that may prove advantageous, and we hold to these things with the passion of a nation whose life depends upon them." He stood up to pace the floor, pausing for a moment in surprise upon finding it bare.

Radovan, absorbed as a child who loves to see an adult give in to a strong emotion, crossed his arms to cup his elbows. "You might give him a quick look at the arsenals," he suggested.

"Shall I scare him?" Eversledge asked the young man, humoringly. "You ought to be scared, you know," he said to Arnold. "It's nothing to be ashamed of. We're scared, too, speaking for myself and the men in the department with me, but fright doesn't cause us to lose our wits. On the contrary, it sharpens them for us. We use our fright constructively." He paused by the window to light a cigarette, then gazed out over the city. "Let's take a glance at the Russian arsenal. They, of course, call it their arsenal for defense. We call it their arsenal for aggression. On land, they've got missile bases numbering in the thousands, mostly bases for intercontinental missiles, 5,000-mile up to 9,000-mile missiles with thermonuclear warheads. In the sea, they've got submarines for launching intermediate-range missiles from submerged points off our coasts. We have no exact count on these subs, but there are enough to cause the whales to wonder. In space, well, they're working on satellites for launching and storage of missiles." He glanced at Arnold. "Are you scared?"

"Very much," replied Arnold readily.

"But wait," said Eversledge, holding up his cigarette between index finger and thumb. He was quick of glance and gesture, a rebound in all his muscles, his entire being focused upon his job. "The arsenal for the defense of the free world is as formidable. We also have our intercontinental missiles and their bases number as many, we believe, as the aggressor's. We, too, have submarines capable of launching intermediate-range missiles from submerged points off the enemy coast. And as for our use of space, we are also developing storage and launching satellites. The formidability of our defense continues even after the entire national society is crippled; it continues in the push-button activating of missiles. Even after everyone is, so to speak, disabled, more missiles can be set off by other blasts or by radiation levels. This is known as 'the push button for the dead man's hand.'" He turned away from the window, came back to press out his cigarette in the chipped glass ash tray, the kind available on drugstore lunch counters. "We are convinced," he said, "that the Russians are prevented from attacking us and our allies by their fear of retaliation, of massive retaliation, by their cognizance that a nuclear war might destroy both sides, a war with no victors. The peace is preserved within the Defense Department in other words. And that's where *you* come in. The Secretary for Humanity, by locating himself with us, makes that fact even more apparent."

Arnold also extinguished his cigarette, their hands at opposite sides of the ash tray signifying concord. After all, he thought, his sitting here at his own desk in this office in the Triangle was a *fait accompli* and so was the nuclear weapons system just described to him and that he was already well aware of from years of newspapers, years of colored photographs in magazines showing missiles departing on experimental flights, and years of books on the subject by statesmen and journalists, sociologists and scientists. And since the parlous times, as he had learned to call them from editorials, existed without doubt, then it followed, did it not, that he must do the best he could from where the times and the President's advisers had put him?

Eversledge, seating himself again, instructed Radovan to phone the pressroom where photographers were waiting, and, laying his dark-sleeved arm along the desk's edge, he addressed himself more closely to Arnold, his manner both urgent and relaxed after the conjoining of their minds. "You'd like a sketch of your day-to-day activity, I'm sure," he said. "You're to be present at disarmament conferences. Not summit, of course, but anything under that, and not in any official capacity, not for the present anyway, but as an observer, a ubiquitous observer. You'll advise, too, of course, but I imagine you'll want to listen and learn first and then make suggestions. The United Nations Disarmament Subcommittee, when it convenes again the middle of this month, will commemorate its tenth year. We think you ought to be there and offer a few words in appreciation of their efforts." He turned his chair toward Arnold, facing him across the desk. "Your first big assignment is just a few days away. Japan. At the Hiroshima Memorial Ceremony you're to deliver a message from our government to the Japanese people. There's been some vociferous opposition there to Japanese rearming, to the missiles we've got there and to the missiles they've got. Japan is an integral part of our "arc" defense against aggression from Asia. It's included in an arc that runs from the Kuril Islands to South Vietnam. We've given Japan a big aid boost to set up her defense program, she's got her own bombs and her own missiles to carry them, and her armed forces are mightier now than they were in the thirties. What you've got to impress upon the nonrealists there—and they always make a big show at the Memorial—is this fact: Japan, by participating in the defense against aggression, participates in preserving the peace. They're afraid that if their country is a missile base, then it'll be a target again, and what you've got to tell them is that if there's a weak link anywhere, we'll all be targets. You can put it in the right words, I'm sure." He stood up as footsteps were heard in the anteroom. "Radovan has some other assignments for you, most of them concerned with civil defense. He'll introduce you to the chairman of our Civil Defense Committee, Skiverveer. His offices are right above you."

The men of the press shuffled through the door with the demeanor of pilgrims entering the bare cell of a holy man. "Not so much reverence!" Radovan cried, enjoying their pantomime, and at once they made themselves at home, as if they were already familiar with the room and regarded its few sticks of furniture and virtuous occupant as public property. Arnold was shunted up against Eversledge, and photographs were taken of them shaking hands. After that, the Secretary of Defense expressed the belief that the potential of Arnold's post would be fulfilled by the man who had been appointed to that post, and Arnold, in his response to that statement, promised the jotting pencils that he would strive to fulfill the expectations of those who had appointed him to this post of meritorious potential.

On the heels of the departing newsmen, Arnold accompanied Eversledge to the door, Radovan leaping swift as a deer to grasp the knob. Clapping the young man on the back, Eversledge said to Arnold, "We don't think you'll have any quarrel with our choice of assistant for you. Came to Washington from Public Relations in New York. One of the best, spent six years at it. But gave it all up for something that satisfies the soul, and nothing does it like Defense Department work." Fondly, he watched Radovan duck his head boyishly and cover his face with his arms in imitation of a prizefighter under blows. "Not only is he competent and conscientious, we thought you'd like him."

When he had closed the door after Eversledge, Radovan turned solicitously to Arnold. "That's enough for one day, don't you think? Tonight you and your family are to dine with Congressman Hal Ribble from your part of the country, and tomorrow there are a number of things scheduled. You're to meet Harringer, that's one thing. So you'd better trot on home now and get some rest." Handing him his hat and opening the door to the outer office and then the door to the anteroom, the energetic young man seemed as proud to be of some slight service to Arnold as he had been in serving their chief.

Arnold hesitated in the anteroom. Something was wanting. That same lack that he had felt back in the apartment began again to plague him. He felt, in his own anteroom, like a solicitor who has sold a magazine subscription by force of charm and, upon turning away, finds that his needs have increased voraciously. An obstinate yearning possessed him to be closer to the President than to Eversledge, though he had accepted the argument for his placement in the Defense Department. Back in the fifties, in the administration before this one, there had been a special adviser to the President, someone with the title of Secretary of Peace, someone grinding away at solving the problems of disarmament. He could not remember his name or what had become of him, but he did recall that the fellow had reported directly to the Chief Executive; and some cynic in him quaked with grim laughter at the picture of that fellow reporting to whoever was Secretary of Defense at that time, with the Chiefs of Staff of the Armed Services also present at that table upon which he spread out his progress report for the disarmament of the nations.

"May I confer with the President if I feel the need?" he asked Radovan.

"You can rest assured that Eversledge will convey all that needs to be conveyed," Radovan said companionably. "I'm sure that Harmon will make every effort to confer with you if you need to see him, but you must remember that he can't take care of everything. Whoever confers with him sifts through reports from subordinates, summarizes, and draws conclusions before he ever knocks on the chamber door. You can imagine the wear and tear on him if everybody got in. Besides, this is an election year and he's swamped. Not only must he carry on with his usual duties, and they're unusual enough in these touchy times, but he's got to campaign as well. So if you don't see him whenever you want to, you'll know it isn't because he doesn't want to see you. Though I suspect he'll want to know why you can't tell the thing, whatever it is, to Eversledge." He leaned a slim shoulder against the door jamb to watch Arnold depart down the hallway. "You know the way home?" he called cheerily.

As he drove home in the dust-gray car which was not many years older than the one he drove in DeVelbiss, Iowa, Arnold pondered upon the insolubility of the times. Under the Triangle roof, military and executive and scientific heads were bent together over the great chart of the nation's defense, and in most of the capitals of the world, groups of the same composition were in continuous session under their own kinds of roofs. If safety lay, as Eversledge had explained, in the formidability of each nation's arsenal, then how and when and where was anyone to begin subtracting from those arsenals? The post he had accepted with the pride of an Eagle Scout became a weight upon his back, became humanity's burden of belligerence, and he forgot all trivial matters, including his aide's direction on how to get home again, losing himself for an hour and more in the maze of streets.

Upon the dim, amber-lit stairs of the apartment house, he was knocked aside by an elderly man whom the landlady was shoving down. Afraid that the old man's sharp bones had bruised her new tenant, the landlady ran down from the top of the flight to dust off Arnold's clothes and pat here and there, apologizing as she bent and bobbed around him. Her victim, hunchbacked by time as if the slovenly years had continued to swing the hammer even after the first blow had bent him the wrong way, lay sprawled on his back on the carpeted stairs, his vacant jaws opening and closing with an indignation too great for words. His suit was covered, it appeared, with verdigris. An old black Homburg remained on his head despite the fall.

"He ain't paid his rent," the landlady explained confidingly, as one managerial mind to another.

"She raised it, the bitch!" cried the old man.

"He ain't cleaned his room in fifty years. And all he does is hawk and spit into old newspapers!" she screamed back, tugging and swatting at Arnold's clothing for emphasis.

"Ask her why was everything fine and dandy before that Secretary for Humanity fool moved in," the tenant cried. "She raised the rent because we got a personality in the house. We got to pay more to hear his toilet flush!"

The old man trying to rise resembled an insect struggling to flip over onto its legs, and Arnold, moved to pity by the sight, grasped a thin arm in the dark, greasy sleeve and lifted him. Again on his feet, the fellow attempted to say more, but his voice failed to rise above the cough climbing it parasitically, like a vine strangling a tree, and grasping the rail with a weak, white hand, he made his shaky descent.

2

At nine in the morning Arnold entered the streams of personnel pouring into the Triangle. The Army sergeant in the booth farthest left who admitted those employees whose surnames began with a letter in the first third of the alphabet examined the identification card that Radovan had given Arnold yesterday.

"Elkins, Sec. for Humanity," said the sergeant under his breath, checking the card against the information contained within a sheaf of papers; then gazing at Arnold's face without seeing the person gazing back whose eyes were described as *hazel*, nose as *aquiline*, and hair as *lt. brown*, he found that everything tallied and gestured for Arnold to enter the lobby.

Quickly halting as several young women crossed in front of him to the bank of elevators on the left of the lobby, and halting again as several young Air Force officers cut across his path to the elevators on the right, he made his way a few steps at a time through the crisscrossing traffic, until he recalled that yesterday his assistant had guided him into the first elevator on the right, for those whose offices were located near the southern angle, and he made his halting way back, entering the assigned elevator at the last moment before one of the several Army officers, already within, pressed the button for the ascent.

Radovan, morning-bright at his desk, which was piled high with letters in plastic letter trays, greeted him by waving a red pencil. "When you put your hat and that death-of-a-salesman's case away, come back out here," he said.

Arnold, closing the door between the offices, sat down and took from his brief case (which *was*, he admitted, rather garish, a russet-colored pigskin case that Becky had given him for Christmas two years ago, but which was, also, seedy now and therefore suitable for his new job) the few small items he had brought from his pitted oak desk at home: a fountain pen and its holder that pivoted on a tiny square of marble; a bronze paperweight lion, the size of a mouse, but heavy, that his mother had given to his father the first time he had won a case in court; and an oval-shaped, winding calendar through whose narrow aperture peered the date, August 1, 1964. After setting these items upon his desk, he opened drawers and, finding them empty, chose the larger one at the bottom for depositing his hat and empty brief case. Then he returned to his assistant's room, rubbing his hands together dryly as one ready to go to work.

Radovan dangled a finger toward a chair by the side of the desk and this Arnold straddled, finding himself before a red tray of letters. "These are some messages that the clerical pool sent up from the thousands they're sorting down there," the young man informed him. "They figured these needed a personal reply and I'm checking the ones that do and sending back the ones that don't. Ever since the post was announced they've been coming in at the rate of a thousand per day. They're all addressed to you, but most of them should have been addressed to fifty other places, such as House committees, Senate committees, Bureau of Standards, Geodetic Survey, Secretary of State, Secretary of Agriculture, Atomic Energy Commission, Surgeon General, and so forth. The public figures you're a catchall for every complaint, every desire. If every letter was yours to answer you'd need sixty secretaries, a couple of hundred clerks, and ninety-nine researchers."

SO NOW YOU THINK YOU ARE GOD? said the telegram on top of Arnold's pile. It was signed by someone he had never met, yet who spoke as if he had watched Arnold for years. He did not regard the post as a means to improve his status, yet the first communication placed in his hands was an accusation. He tossed the telegram aside.

"We won't be doing this every day," Radovan said. "The girls will get better at it and send up fewer. This is nothing, though, compared to the mail received a couple of months ago when Congress was considering the Otten-hauser-Riley bill enabling pets—cats and dogs and monkeys, if you've got one—to accompany their owners into the public shelters. Support for the measure came from millions of individuals and thousands of organizations, secular and religious." With his pencil he checked a letter and placed it on another pile. "Let me explain the procedure," he said. "We've got, roughly, three categories of communications. There's one category—everything from postcards to petitions to treatises—from persons warning of nuclear calamity, an end of the world, etc., etc., and presenting their formulas for saving the world. What they imply, usually, is that we get down on our knees to the enemy. We've got a form letter for that category, one that commends them for seeking peace and reiterates the truism that our military strength will prevent the war they so absorbingly fear. Once in a while, one of these frantic communications is from somebody with a name. In that case, we don't send the form letter, we put the answer differently—a theme with variations, you know—and you sign it personally, no rubber stamp. Then there's category two, like this one," he said, tapping with his pencil another pile of letters. "They need specific answers, saying either that there's nothing you can do and you're sorry or referring the writer to somebody else. This one, for instance, is from a woman, a widow, relating the fatal shooting of her husband by a person or persons unknown during a rush to stake out claims to uranium deposits in South Dakota and requesting compensation for the loss of his life in the service of his country. Don't worry yourself about the answer; I'll advise the clerical pool what to say," he said, noticing Arnold's troubled gaze. "We'll take up the third category now, because you're due, in a few minutes, to pose for press photos with the writer of this particular letter in that category, the president of the Ecstasy Chocolate Bar Company."

Arnold took the letter bearing at the top the embossed name of the firm and the picture of a candy bar emerging from a red wrapper. The letter complained of the monopolistic practice of a nation-wide grocery chain in promoting its own brand of chocolate bar for emergency ration kits. The kits, the president reminded him, were prominently displayed at every store in the chain. They were of plastic in a variety of colors and sizes, and they contained the store's brand of canned meats, whole wheat wafers, powdered milk, and chocolate bars. The complainant told of his request for a conference with the management, desiring, he said, to impress upon those gentlemen the value of variety. More kits would be sold if other brands of chocolate bars were also displayed within them. But to date no reply had been received. He had written, also, to the Civil Defense Committee of the Department of Defense, as their endorsement of the kits was tantamount to endorsing all products on display within them, but in their reply the Committee had denied this allegation. The letter ended with an appeal to Arnold to intervene. "It's infinitesimal," Arnold said, returning the letter to his assistant's outstretched hand.

"What is?" Radovan inquired, his pliable eyebrows puzzled.

"Whether you've got a candy bar in your kit when the alarm sounds."

"But chocolate is a source of energy," Radovan explained, "and even the unwrapping of a candy bar while you're sitting deep in a shelter is an act of affirmation."

"There's *something* there that doesn't matter," Arnold insisted.

"I disagree with you," said Radovan. "You can't always think of humanity in the abstract, you know. Where's your sympathy for the individual? Here's a man with a wife and children, no doubt, and a business he wants to see prosper, for his family's sake and for the sake of a healthy national economy. Besides, when you search for a solution to one man's problem you may find that it's a solution a lot of men can use and have been waiting for. This letter got to Washington before you did, and it struck me as so important that I ran up and had a talk with Skiverveer, chairman of the Civil Defense Committee. Kits, you know, are a product of the dispersal or evacuation phase of civil defense, when we had enough time to take off for the mountains or the country. Everyone was urged to keep nine-day rations in the trunk of the car, or twelve-day, whatever it was. But dispersal is losing advocates, because even if we had enough time to disperse we can't escape the fallout in a big attack. So there's no place to go but down. Well, we figured that now we're getting our shelters, we'll need dispensing machines for several kinds of things like canned meat, hot coffee, candy, everything the kits have in them. It saves lugging food down with you. All you need is the money in your pocket. Of course, those who want to bring their kits can, but for those who don't or can't—this is the answer. So I picked up the phone and Skiverveer and myself talked with Ecstasy's president in St. Louis and he agreed to drop by today and have his picture taken with you and Skiverveer. You'll be shaking his hand and thanking him for spurring further exploration of the problem of nourishment in the shelters." He grinned chidingly at Arnold. "So it isn't as infinitesimal as you think, is it?"

"Somewhere in the edifice is a crack," Arnold said, "though I can't put my finger on it any more." Since there was no other place to rest his elbow, he rested it on a pile of letters and rubbed the corrugations from his brow.

A phone call from the sergeant at the visitors' booth interrupted the further sorting of letters. Radovan put a call through to Skiverveer, informing him that the Ecstasy president was on his way up, and these two gentlemen entered the anteroom at the same time. They were welcomed into the office by Radovan, who introduced himself to the visitor (a fellow impeccably attired, and also somewhat nervous, his argument still ready inside his cheeks, for it was the logic of it that had impressed these men in the upper reaches of government), and introduced the visitor to Arnold and to Skiverveer, a portly young man who appeared to be out of breath from demonstrating, down the stairs and corridor, the swiftness of his reactions.

"The press is to meet us at the Greely Street excavation," Skiverveer explained. "Work's just beginning there, and Elkins, here, can help dig the first shovelful, so to speak. A kind of ceremony, with Ecstasy, here, to the left and myself to the right, or vice versa. My car is waiting," he said, gripping Arnold's arm.

"Perhaps we'd better use Elkins' car," Radovan suggested. "He's what you might call the spiritual guide of the excursion. He can drive, and I'll direct him because I know the streets."

The three of them waited for Arnold to precede them, and this he did, but with the feeling that he was pushed forward by a line of guards.

"It does seem odd to me," he said, as they waited at the curb for the parking attendant to bring his car, "that I am called upon to participate in this shelter scene. My job, as I understand it, is to see that this nation never descends, my job is to see that the alarm never sounds."

The parking attendant slipped agilely away from the clutching plush upholstery of the driver's seat and threw open the rear door. Radovan invited the president of Ecstasy Chocolate to enter first and followed him in, Arnold got into the driver's seat, and Skiverveer settled down beside him, rocking side to side on his haunches as if avoiding a broken spring.

"That would have made a good question a year ago," Skiverveer said, "before civil defense was recognized, really recognized, as a vital link in the defense of the nation. Where were you when Eversledge called on Congress for that giant Federal survey to examine all the cellars and sewers and mines and determine which ones to outfit as public fallout shelters and also to determine just where to construct some other mass shelters? I talked myself blue in the face at those congressional committee hearings when we were asking for appropriations for the survey and, again, when we were asking for funds to construct the shelters that the survey said we ought to have. All the anti-Administration congressmen firing questions at me about expense, about cement—did we have enough or would the shelters take it away from other industry? Anything to sabotage it. What they wanted to do was postpone it, postpone the whole damn shelter program until after elections this year. And then if their own party got control, they could claim that shelter program as their very own, make a whopping big thing out of it." His voice was hard and edgy, as if it had fallen into the habit of sparring with anyone resembling an interrogator.

Arnold, turning a corner as he was ordered to do by Radovan's rear-seat voice, admitted to himself that he was less amenable than he ought to be to the nation's shelter program. He recalled the day the excavation crew had begun to dig the DeVelbiss public shelter in the park across from the campus. It had been the first day of summer vacation, and he had gone to his office at the college to collect his papers and books and to chat awhile with students, prepared to give a kind of gentle, worldly counseling to those graduating students who were not returning. But on that day, at eight o'clock exactly, the bulldozers began to fell the trees, the jackhammers began to jump, and the noise was so overriding that all he could do for his visiting students was shout homilies at them. Later in the morning he had gone over to the park to watch the machines. Standing under the trees, he watched the jackhammers cracking away the concrete square upon which bands had marched, charity carnivals had twirled their colored lights, and students had danced away the proms of many summer nights; cracking away the elaborate fountain with its Grecian jar carriers and its low broad pedestal around which so many children, including his own, had run untiring circles; and he watched the trees around the square toppling before the yellow bulldozers, their leafy tops shaking with a fearful palsy. He had felt consumed by the uproar, and it had seemed to him that the spectators, the men at work—all were engaged in a mindless vandalism. Then the appearance of a foreman, flapping his hat at the spectators to force them back, had reminded him that he was witnessing the implementation of an Act of Congress. The lawmakers had sent machinery striking into the earth, ripping up parks and streets and city blocks all over the country, preparing a descent for the citizens in the event of nuclear war. Dejected, he had returned to his desk and shaken the cement dust from his hair. "I suppose," he said to Skiverveer, "I have a psychological barrier against going underground. It's always meant the end of everything to me," and he smiled at his own humor.

Skiverveer flung his arm over the back of the seat, pulling himself around so that he could glare at Radovan. "My God, man!" he cried. "You call him Secretary for Humanity and he says something like that? It'll be the end of us if we *don't* go down, believe me!" Afraid that Arnold's profile could not hear as well as his complete face, he raised his voice. "Before the shelter program, experts from the Kalt Corporation—they figure out anything you ask them to—estimated that in a saturation missile attack upon this nation we'd stand to lose a good part of our 180 million population if we had no civil defense. They'd die from blast, heat, prompt radiation, fallout, and disruption of our food and medical supply system. Now that civil defense has come into its own, now that the public realizes that their best buy is shelters, we can expect to cut that number way, way down." He began to count off on his fingers. "They're not foolproof, but what is? Take the first —blast. There's no shelter going to withstand blast, we can't go that deep; and they're not going to withstand heat, either; and that prompt radiation gets in through as much as two feet of concrete anywhere within a diameter of four miles under the explosion. In other words, you can't expect too much of them under a direct hit, and a direct hit takes in quite a bit. But they'll serve as fallout protection, a place to stay put until the blanket of radiation clears off the continent, and there'll be food down there and medical supplies. We're working it out to the last detail to try to save as many lives as possible, and you sit there and call yourself Secretary for Humanity and scoff at saving half the population. My God, that's ninety million lives you'd be throwing away just because you had a psychological barrier against shelters." He jerked himself forward again. "It's this you've got to remember," he said, pulling out a package of cigarettes. "If the enemy knows that we've got enough foresight to save a substantial part of our population, why that's part of our deterrence strategy. Say we got down to half, say we saved half, that's what the population was in 1910, and with that kind of a figure we can bound to our feet again. If it's your job to see that the bombs don't fall, then you'll be doing that job by enforcing our deterrence strategy, by going out and doing what you're going to do at the Greely Street shelter."

"Turn left," said Radovan from the rear seat.

But confused by Skiverveer's ringing voice in his ear, Arnold signaled for a right turn and made the turn. The car was now in a stream of traffic that was detoured away from the excavation site, and as he readily accepted his assistant's advice on how to maneuver into a lane that gave him access to a turn-off, he accepted, also, the thesis argued by Skiverveer, and was appalled by the callousness of his conflict with the shelter program.

When, at the shelter fence, photographers placed a yellow helmet on his head and a jackhammer in his hands, Arnold did not argue, although he could not bring himself to smile. Skiverveer, smiling, stood at his left and the Ecstasy president at his right, unsmiling, overwhelmed, no doubt, by the response to his letter, his increased prestige pulling down his cheeks like lead weights. Then, with helmet and hammer removed, another photo was taken of Arnold shaking hands with the Ecstasy president while Skiverveer looked approvingly on. When all was over, Radovan hailed a taxi and after much shaking of hands, Skiverveer and the honored visitor climbed into the taxi to return to the Triangle and Arnold and Radovan, the latter claiming the driver's seat, drove on to the White House for the meeting with Harmon Harringer.

A press conference was in progress when they arrived. They were ushered in through one of several doors by a gray-haired Presidential aide who shook hands with Arnold as if extremely pleased to make his acquaintance. A reporter amidst the many who were seated in an arc before the President's desk was framing a question pertaining to foreign policy, and when the President had answered it, his aide informed him, in a low voice, that Arnold Elkins, the Secretary for Humanity, had arrived. The President, clasping Arnold's hand, introduced him to the press.

"Elkins is from Iowa," he reminded them, standing close to Arnold like a father proud of his son who measures three inches taller than himself, and, his sand-gray head still nodding agreeably at his appointee, he began to reminisce about his own boyhood, as the son of a drayer in Shanosaw County, Ohio. "My grandfather had horses, dray horses," he said. "Horses were an integral part of the American scene. But my father had a truck, and by the time I was sixteen years old he had a team of trucks. My brother Shelby, who operates the business now, has trucks the size of which my father never imagined, and he's planning on jet freight in the not too distant future." He put his hand on Arnold's shoulder. "Times change," he said. "Twenty years ago, ten years ago, such a post as Secretary for Humanity would have been inappropriate, but today it's a job necessitated by the extraordinary times. My brother requires jet freight to cope with the industrial growth of the country. In the sphere of government, a Secretary for Humanity is required to cope with the nuclear age. It's a job of great magnitude, a new magnitude we can say. The peoples of the world are awestruck by our great missile system, by the number and range of our missiles, and by the destructive capacity of the bombs that they carry. They need constant sight of the meaning behind these weapons, weapons the like of which the world has never known. This post of Secretary for Humanity, this man chosen to fill it, says clearly to the peoples of the world that if we must arm ourselves it is only because we are morally obligated to do so. We will not be coerced, we will not be blackmailed, we will not be forced to the wall by the threats of the aggressor. We say to them, we resist your threat with a weapons system that matches and surpasses your own because it is a moral obligation upon us. Our weapons are the equipment of a moral force, a moral force that cannot be extinguished. When the enemy is made aware of this force, and we hope it will not take him over-long, he will be compelled to co-operate with us on a system of disarmament that will, ultimately, free the peoples of the world from the fear of nuclear war." His hand slipped down from Arnold's shoulder, coming to rest above his elbow. "Arnold Tennyson Elkins, our Secretary for Humanity, is our missile-age envoy to all the world's peoples."

There was some flashing of bulbs as he shook hands with Harringer. "Elkins commenting?" someone asked from the rear.

Arnold ran his index finger along the edge of the highly polished walnut desk at his right hand. "The sentence that I found particularly gratifying in President Harringer's letter to me was this—that some day all nations will sit down together and enjoy the fruits that this nuclear age has yet to offer. It is my hope that in my capacity as Secretary for Humanity I will be of some influence in bringing this feast about, and in the not distant future. A man could ask for no task more worth while, more rewarding, and I am happy to have been chosen for the assignment." Lifting his eyes, he found some newsmen jotting down his words and others listening as they were rising from their chairs or moving toward the door.

The President cleared his throat, and all eyes turned to him again and all shuffling ceased. "It's fine to quote him," he said, throwing his voice outward to gather in the farthest of the departing group, "but I'd like to add a word. Yes, some day we may sit down together, the nations of the world, but we must be careful, this country must be careful not to sit down too soon. We must be wary of partaking of that which may be offered to us by our table companion lest that fruit be poisoned and we perish. We will pray for that feast and we will work for it, but we will not sit down until we are convinced of the good will of all those who are celebrating at that table." Clapping Arnold a last clap on the shoulder, the President strode out a door held open for him by his aide, who, before he turned to follow, gave Arnold a friendly salute, swinging two fingers to his temple.

They followed the men and women of the press down the corridor. "His comment on beware the poisoned fruit made me feel like Snow White," Arnold complained to his assistant. "I am as aware as the next man of the need to be cautious."

"Harmon is wise," Radovan replied. "The Russians aren't that easy to sit down with. At every conference they make trouble from the word go. You made it sound easy."

They climbed into the car again, Radovan choosing to drive, and as Arnold fumbled for a match while his cigarette hung from his lips, his assistant brought forth his paper-thin lighter and flicked up the steady little flame, all with an easy, graceful movement of his right hand while his left hand remained competently on the steering wheel, a favor that did not calm and console the recipient, as it was probably intended to do, but instead increased his sense of failure.

"I'm going to drop myself off at the Triangle," Radovan said as they neared the building, "and you drive on home because there's a young lady visiting with your wife and daughters and she wants to make your acquaintance, too. She's got a request to make of the family." Alighting before the Triangle and slamming the car door, he saluted Arnold as the Presidential aide had saluted him, two fingers jauntily to the temple, a sign of optimism and good feelings, an admonition not to bow his poor novice's head under the weight of a very small criticism.

At the entrance to the apartment building, a shining, middle-priced, three-toned automobile was parked, and Arnold maneuvered his car in behind it. Up in the apartment, a young woman was seated on the lumpy sofa—an extremely pretty, quick-smiling young woman in a blue summer dress, white sandals with heels long and slender as pencils, and a small white straw hat loaded with bachelor buttons. Her name, said Alma, introducing her, was Marybeth Crockett, and, shaking hands with her, Arnold noticed at close range the many small perfections of her person and her blossom-light perfume. She was, he thought, the embodiment of a precious summer one envisions from advertisements of couples on a beach, or picnicking on some grass by the front fender of the kind of car parked by the apartment house entrance.

"But you're exactly right!" she cried, gazing up at him. "Tall and lean, a little bit gauche and a lot of natural dignity. There's something real grassroots about you!"

Seating himself across the coffee table from her, he took in at a glance his family's response to her. Bernice, standing behind her mother's chair, was so impressed that she could not take her eyes away; Becky had folded herself far back in a large chair and, narrowing her eyes and plucking at her lower lip, she observed the effects of the visitor upon her sister; while Alma, forced to compare herself with the visitor because of Miss Crockett's perfection, felt her imperfections obvious in her hostess's smile. The seventh daughter of an unprosperous farmer, Alma had worked her way through the state university's music department and her fame as a piano teacher brought students from all over Langshank County, but sometimes, in the presence of women like Marybeth Crockett, she lost her vigorous ways and became as her mother might have been when trapped in the farm kitchen by a city woman visiting—became suspicious, crabbed, contrary. She poured tea for the guest from the landlady's large brown teapot, chipped at the spout.

"As I was telling your family," Miss Crockett said, "you

can call me the Washington *liaison man*"—laughing at
the designation as lyrically as if they had all laughed together over other things many times before—"for Nord
and Nicholas Advertising Agency. And I can't remember
when I've enjoyed an assignment more, because I'm involved up to here"—touching the seed pearls at her throat
—"in defense work. The project that I'm working on is going to save millions of lives, and can you imagine a job
more satisfying than that? And I came here to persuade
you and your family to share that job with me."

"She was talking about a problem when you came in,"
Becky said in a flat voice.

"The problem was this," said Miss Crockett, eager to
take up where she had left off. "Although the U.S. Printing Office has, for a number of years now, run off its presses
millions of copies of civil defense pamphlets, there were
no takers. Stacks of them were available free at post offices
and public libraries, but they remained there. With the
shelter program digging in, something new was absolutely
needed, a whole new concept of a civil defense pamphlet.
So James Eversledge, our Secretary of Defense, called into
conference his Civil Defense Committee along with three
eminent psychologists and three top-bracket men in moti-
vation research, the study of what makes people buy. Well,
it was decided at that conference that one of the big reasons why the pamphlets didn't move was a lack of a felt
need for them in the public mind. The solution, of course,
was that civil defense must become a product. But that
isn't as simple as it sounds. Before civil defense can come
into its own as a compelling and ethical product, it must
first be associated with a popular product or products,
proved to be all that the makers claim. Nord and Nicholas
chose their White Cloud Detergent account to team up
with civil defense because it's one of their consistent best

sellers, and other agencies are running ads combining the product message with a civil defense message, such as, Buy two cans, put one in your shelter. But I tend to like the White Cloud idea best because of its scope." And she leaned forward to tap a pink-tipped finger on a booklet lying on Alma's lap.

It was, he saw, a brightly colored booklet, its cover bordered with the popularized diagram of the chain reaction of the fission process, a diagram resembling balloons on sticks, and he understood why Bernice was leaning on the back of her mother's chair.

Alma held the booklet away at arm's length as if she were farsighted with age, as if age had also deprived her of a quick reception of the younger woman's lively, learned presence. "She says it's all about how to survive an H-bomb attack," Alma told him, squintingly.

"Open it, open it, Mama!" Bernice urged, and, leaning forward, her long hair trailing against her mother's cheek and her arm crossing her mother's bosom, she opened the booklet herself.

Miss Crockett crossed her knees as a teacher clasps her hands together upon the desk and begins a lecture. "It tells us how to use all our shelters," she explained. "For example, in the public-shelter section, it advises us to memorize the quickest way to get to the closest ones and how to behave when we're down inside. Another section is for suburban shelters. Some housing developments already have their shelters, installed by thoughtful developers, and really a selling point for the houses. One I know of has mahogany paneling over the concrete walls and is used as a recreation room in rainy weather—ping-pong tables and everything. This particular section tells tract dwellers, for instance, how to work with their neighbors in putting in supplies in the tract shelter and how to organize a roundup of kids. There are suggestions, also, for non-tract families. For example, the kind of shelter you build is dictated by your income and the terrain of your property. At the back of the booklet there's a section on how to use the radiation meters that the government is to distribute to each family to enable them to tell when it's safe to come up again."

"Why is everybody smiling?" Alma asked as Bernice turned the pages.

"That's the way Adam Ize draws people," Miss Crockett replied, amazed that Alma was not familiar with the artist's cartoons.

"I mean, why did they give *him* the job?" Alma asked.

"Never underestimate the sophistication of the public," said Miss Crockett admonishingly. "The U.S. Printing Office pamphlets had those uninspired line drawings of a family preparing to enter their back-yard shelter. You know—Mother carrying a basket, Father turning off the pilot light under the water heater, Junior carrying a radio, and little Susan a flashlight. But we chose Ize. He has caught on with the public because, as one critic put it in an analysis of his art, he is honest and we are not, and his honesty lies in his bold recognition of the pleasure that comes from the macabre. His people, no matter what kind of grisly task they're engaged in, always have a lurking smile. That smile is a philosophy, one that accepts all that living has to offer, including an end of living. It's the most profound kind of Togetherness with Life. The funniest cartoon is that smiling little man dragging his coffin down the public shelter steps."

"How may we help you with your job?" Arnold asked, hoping, with his courteous awareness of her needs, to allay the effect of his wife's and younger daughter's affectation of rural idiocy.

"She wants to put a picture of the family on the first

page," Becky said, "and across from it she wants an inspirational message signed by all of us."

Alma closed the booklet with her daughter's hand still in it and bent forward to lift the teapot cover and peer inside. "It doesn't seem to me that we're the right family for the job," she said. She nodded in Arnold's direction. "They told him to see that there wouldn't be a war."

She was following a step behind him, Arnold thought. Her objection was the same he had put to Skiverveer, and her comprehension was to come now, a few hours after his own. And he visualized himself coming in out of the hinterlands, with her following him ploddingly, like a squaw.

"Of course there won't!" cried the young woman, her voice the kind that dispels bears from a child's bedroom. "And this booklet is going to help prevent it. With our shelter system, our big ones and all the little ones all over the nation, the enemy won't be able to panic us or demoralize us or break our spirit, no matter what they do. What we've got to remember," she said, shaking her white gloves in gentle reminder, "is not to think about the morning after a thermonuclear attack. We've got to think in terms of ten years after, because if we've got half or more of our population, by that time we'll be on the way to getting back to where we were. We'll still be a strong, free nation." She looked toward Arnold for corroboration.

"Skiverveer gave me the figures," Arnold assured her, nodding.

Alma handed up the teapot to Bernice, behind her. "The tea is cold," she said. "Will you heat some water, please?"

"Mama, are you going to say yes?" Bernice pleaded, her face mottled with the shame of her relationship to her sister and her mother. The White Cloud booklet, Arnold thought, is the answer to her prayers, and Miss Marybeth Crockett, the angel that winged it down to her.

Alma drank her cold tea cautiously, pursing her lips to blow upon it. "I never did go in for giving thanks that I was spared in flood or fire or tornado when others lost out," she said. "There's something not right about it. The way I feel, if there's going to be half the people saved I'd rather not be among them, because I'd think too much about the half that wasn't there." The teacup rattled in the saucer as she set it down on the table. Somewhat gingerly, as if it were a dead crane fly, she picked up the book from her lap and returned it to the visitor. "It's nothing I'd be interested in, I guess."

Jerking away, Bernice caught her foot under the dining-room rug and the teapot flew from her hands and broke on the floor. Her sobs broke as the crockery broke. A strange house grows more familiar, Arnold thought, when one watches a member of the family flee to a bedroom.

Miss Crockett got to her sandaled feet as graciously, as smilingly, as if all that she had asked of them had been granted her, and after expressing her appreciation of their hospitality, she left, guided by Arnold down the stairs.

"Can you persuade her?" she asked, pulling on her gloves in the tiled entry.

"She has always voted independently of me," he replied. They had always agreed, his wife and he, in the area of politics, yet he felt that in spite of Miss Crockett's erudition, she could apply this old-fashioned complaint with more ease than she could any other explanation he might give her.

"It is, you must admit, a peculiar callousness," she said. "If we can't save all, she wants to save none." Musing upon the absurdity of his wife's reason for refusing her request, she drove away, remembering in time to wave at him a small, white-gloved, sympathetic hand.

He climbed back up the stairs, two steps at a time, his

anger against his family climbing within him. All day, and yesterday, the theory of deterrence had been explained to him by some of its leading exponents and he had comprehended the logic of it. Only an hour ago, donning a yellow helmet and shaking hands with a jackhammer, he had participated in a great country-wide project, playing his small part in saving half and more of the people of the nation. But Alma's emphasis upon the other half, the unsaved half, roused again his own doubting, which scratched at this theory like a mole tunneling inside. *She* was a mole. She had eyes like a mole's when it came to perceiving the complexities of the nuclear age. The fact that Bernice had seen the necessity for the booklet gave him no satisfaction; he wanted no alliance with someone who was so desperately susceptible to promises from pretty people. On reaching the door, he ground the knob around with such force that a tiny, blackish screw shot out from the stem.

Alma was on her knees, gathering up the teapot fragments, and Becky was clearing away the cups. He began to roam the room, picking up cushions and tossing them down again, wanting words to explain to moles all that had been explained to him since that first ride to the Triangle, wanting vigorous words that would convey the vigor of the theoreticians, so that they would know that persons other than Miss Crockett had proved to him the value of her handy disaster booklet with the balloons on the cover.

Becky piled one cup upon another, holding the tower against her chest. "What you could do," she suggested, "is let them put our family's picture in the book but let Mama and myself turn our backs. You know how they take pictures of people in prisons or mental institutions, they let you see the warden or the nurse, but all you can see of the inmate is the back of his head? So when they get out they won't be stigmatized?" She was afraid of him in his agitation, averting her eyes but unable to keep the last word to herself.

He found a limp cushion in his hands and slammed it down into the chair he had sat in. "My advice to you," he shouted at her, "is this: Write a letter to the New York *Times*. Say it this way; say: 'Dear Sir, I am thirteen years old. I have figured out an answer to the H-bomb problem. All the countries stop making them. Everybody stop. Then everything will be all right again. Yours sincerely, Becky Elkins.'" He strode into the dining room on his way to the bedroom, but remembering that Bernice had retired to that region a few minutes earlier, he swept up his hat from the table and strode to the door. Alma still on her knees reminded him of someone cowering, and the resemblance made a tyrant of him.

In a hole-in-the-wall café, several blocks away, he slid into a red plastic booth, and while he drank bitter coffee he wrote his speech for Japan on the back of the President's envelope that he found in the inside pocket of his coat, writing it also for Alma, to enlighten her. And there was something enjoyably predictive about his working it out on the back of an envelope in a café of noisy customers and spattering grease, as if someday it were to be a document in the archives of famous words on scraps of paper, words written in humility by a speaker underestimating their importance.

3

The family was flown to Japan by the Military Air Transport Service. The plane was crowded with Army men returning to the Far East from furloughs in the States, and a young master sergeant, boarding at San Francisco, sat down next to Arnold who was sitting by himself, still at odds with his wife. Alma sat next to an Army nurse, and the girls also sat apart, each claiming a window seat. As night spread over the ocean, Arnold, his head back upon his pillow, chatted with the sergeant who, desirous of exploiting the presence of a cabinet member, recounted the subterfuges of his girl friend and his own cunning strategy in unmasking her. After an hour Arnold cut in with an inquiry about the city of Hiroshima at whose U.S. air base the sergeant was stationed.

"I hear," he said, "that it's a beautiful city now, new architecture . . ."

". . . new parks," the soldier continued, his head back on his pillow. "Nice wide streets . . ."

"The same thing in Nagasaki?"

"Never been to Nagasaki," the soldier replied, stretching his legs sleepily now that he was no longer the subject of conversation. "Never heard much about Nagasaki, did you? Maybe because it came second, it lost out on being the first city ever to get an atomic bomb. Never been to Nagasaki."

Arnold tried to sleep, reclining on his side, facing the aisle. Some soldiers were snoring and others were talking together in low voices. His shoulder felt pinched and he shifted it around until he was less uncomfortable. The trouble with Alma, he said to himself, she had an overdeveloped conscience as some women have overdeveloped breasts and some men overdeveloped biceps, and she was proud of the deformity. She held herself responsible to right an injustice as far away as South Africa, and sensed always around her those injustices she would never hear about, and what she exacted of herself she exacted of others. She demanded of her husband in his new capacity that he put an end to the enmity among nations with the very force of his will. He knew her well enough to know that this was what she had in mind for him to do. The thousand roots of one event, the terrifying, cumulative weight of history on humanity, on a nation, on the leaders of the nation, on her own husband—this she failed to see. Her conscience made her shortsighted, it made a mole of her.

He flung himself over, as he sometimes flung himself away from her in bed after an argument, and facing the sleeping soldier, began again his criticism of her; but the sergeant suddenly flapped his elbow at something, muttering a curse, and Arnold silenced his thoughts, believing that their stridency was disturbing the young man's sleep.

The U.S. consul at Hiroshima met the plane. He was a slight and dapper fellow of sixty or so, with wispy wings of gray hair above his ears. Ushering the Elkins family into his small, steel-gray car, he explained humorously that he preferred a small car in order to make room on the island for the larger ones shipped over from the States. As the car moved off the base, Arnold saw that the highway ahead of them was lined with men, women, and children carrying signs with the words BAN THE BOMB.

"They knew of your arrival in advance," the consul said. "What day, what hour. You'll see them on the sidewalk by the hotel. I saw them on my way here. But wait until tomorrow, the sixth of August. The way they're starting out, they may get out of hand. Personally," he said, with two nervous fingers smoothing his thin mustache, "I think it was a mistake to send you. Why Harringer thinks he's got to make a big thing of it with a Secretary for Humanity— If you ask me, any senator could get it across, somebody whose title doesn't mean the things that yours does."

The entrance to the hotel was obscured by sign-bearing crowds. The way was cleared for the Elkins family and the consul by twelve policemen, and they entered a luxurious lobby of long, persimmon-red couches, heavy brass ash trays on low, black tables, and a thick sand-color rug—a lobby that repelled the sound of hundreds of shuffling feet outside the door.

"Your assistant instructed me to find rooms for you at some third-rate hotel, but that doesn't make sense," he said as their few small suitcases were carried past them to the elevator by two bellboys in white silk pants and jackets. "This is where anybody who is anybody puts up. If they want you to put up somewhere else, they don't take into account that after you're gone I'm still in the city, and some of the respect the people here give me would be taken away if you, a government executive, registered at some flophouse."

The consul escorted them to their suite, then left them so that they could rest, informing them that supper would be brought up at six and that he would return at that time to dine with them. The family, the silence among them intensified by the long trip and by the shock of their importance to the crowds below, freshened up in the tiled bathrooms and lay down for naps upon low beds covered with silken spreads.

At six the consul returned, followed by two Japanese girls in kimonos pushing a food cart. The family sat down on cushions and ate from fragile dishes on a low, lacquered table. When the waitresses had left, Arnold, who felt undeserving of their constant smiles, commented, "They're the only ones among all I've seen who ask for nothing but approval."

The consul picked up a pink shrimp with his ebony chopsticks and popped it into his mouth. "You can say that it was quite a traumatic experience, the bomb," he said. "It seems to have distorted their view of reality, as traumas do. They can't—a considerable number of them, that is— they can't seem to take in the imperative need of including Japan in the defense of the free world." He shrugged, drew to himself his bowl of rice, and fluffed it up with his chopsticks. "As you will see, they come from all over Japan to these Hiroshima Memorials to indicate their unwillingness. They can't seem to accept the deterrence theory—

the more missiles the less possibility of war. That's why *you're* here," he said, glancing up, his large, moisty brown eyes affable and encouraging. But one eyelid flickered involuntarily, a derisive flicker, and for a moment Arnold saw the consul not as a consul but as an ancient Japanese host, seated on a cushion with a bowl of rice held within the concavity of his chest, a host whose code of deportment forbade him to disagree with a guest, but who disagreed anyway, with signals of excessive praise and the dropping of an eyelid. At once the consul engaged Alma in conversation, recalling the pleasant details of his visit last spring to his daughter and her children in Syracuse, New York.

After supper, the consul sat with Arnold on the long white couch and described the ceremony that was to take place in the morning. He said that the copy of the speech that Arnold had given him that afternoon was in the hands of the Mayor of Hiroshima, who was to translate it into Japanese following Arnold's delivery of it in English. "It's pure poetry," the consul said, shaking his head admiringly.

Arnold accepted the praise, adding it to that he had received from Radovan. The prospect, early in the morning, of his small, foreign presence beside a great memorial arch for the multitudinous dead filled him with such misgivings that he was forced to embrace this accumulated praise to warm himself. When the consul had left, and he and his family lay upon their silken beds, he read the speech again with his mind's eye and it was lambently illuminated by the response it had stirred.

At seven he was wakened by the quick rustling of covers as Alma sat up in the bed next to his, sat upright out of sleep.

"What time did the bomb fall?" he asked her.

"Eight-fifteen," she told him.

He already knew the hour of the bomb but he had asked her in order to bridge the gap between them with a shared comprehension of the day, for in this first moment of his awakening he saw that the words he had prepared were wanting. What was he doing here, lying on his back under silken covers, his praiseworthy little speech on the tip of his tongue? He had no business promising that the bomb would never fall when it had already fallen.

He threw back his covers and strode to the window to look down upon the park. The consul had told him that they began coming before dawn, mourners from the city and mourners from all Japan. He saw them streaming in, laying their wreaths before the arch and planting their incense sticks, bowing their prayers, and mingling with the rest who were waiting for the ceremony to begin. Farther out he saw the huge, grassy mound that contained the ashes of the unknown dead. It rose higher than the men and women who clustered by it, observing the ritual of Buddhist priests, Shinto priests, Christian clergymen, all whom the consul had named last night with a swift tongue. Around the park, the city sent up its morning mists into a clear sky. Yesterday, from this window and with the consul at his side, he had seen it as a city rising again from ashes, a feat that he had marveled at and accepted, as resurrections are sometimes accepted as a matter of course. But now he saw it as a city whose destruction was coming. For in the almost twenty years that the particular city of Hiroshima was rising again—while the blueprints were drawn, the frameworks built, the stones laid, the doors hung—at the same time the number of bombs was increasing. The day the first one had fallen they could be counted on the fingers of the hand. Now there were thousands, now there were tens of thousands, and the terror in their cube roots was immeasurably more than in that early one. He heard his wife's bare footsteps, and when she came up beside him he put his arm around her in the hope of conveying to her that when he delivered his speech he himself would know, as well as his audience, that his voice was the voice of a pebble in the sound of the inferno that was to come.

The consul knocked at seven-thirty, dressed in a black suit of lightweight cloth, a suit appropriate both for the hot weather and the day of mourning. They were again escorted through the sidewalk crowds, stepped into his car, and were driven to the parking area reserved for participants in the ceremony. Upon the temporary platform before the arch the consul introduced the family to the Mayor, then ran lightly down as a stagehand runs from the curtain's parting. With the Mayor on the platform stood the Governor of the Prefecture and a brother of the Emperor, with his wife. Arnold, lifting his eyes, found the density of the crowd and the size of it frightening. They filled the park. No less, he thought, than fifty thousand, and the only sounds he heard were the voices of small children twittering like birds in a forest and, far in the sky, the roar of a jet squadron streaking north.

At the stroke of eight, church and temple bells began their various tollings, a sound that emanated from the entire city. The choir's song, the Governor's speech, each seemed to Arnold like a chant of lament, more affecting because the words were strange. The ascent of the doves, at the moment of the bomb, preceded Arnold's participation. They rose so swiftly they seemed to have been flung against the sky, and the whirring of their wings was the kind of sound that, even after it is gone, one hesitates to interrupt. The Mayor introduced him and he spoke, his voice converted by the public address system into a giant's voice, breaking and echoing against the inside of the metal casing that the sky had become. He stepped back to his family's side again and listened to the Mayor translate the speech into Japanese. Under the high arch the Emperor's brother and his wife placed a wreath upon the casket containing the names of those persons known to have perished in the bombing. The consul gave a wreath to Arnold and his wife to place among the others piled before the arch and gave incense sticks to the girls to set into the earth, and when the family had done this, he led them away.

As they moved through the breaking crowd, from all around them rose the sound of thousands of wings rustling, and they saw that almost every person was taking from his pocket a paper sign that, unfolded, read BAN THE BOMB. Several men who had pressed close upon the car jumped back as the car slid away, and a sign fell against Arnold's window, tapping frantically at the pane.

"This is the first time they've pulled signs at the ceremony," the consul said. "All I can say is, they waited long enough to do it." He smiled wryly. "The tourists from the States will say, of course, the Japanese are so clever with paper tricks!"

They had driven only a few feet when a sheet of paper swished against the windshield, followed by several more against the windows. The consul braked the car. More papers came swerving and drifting down, ten more and fifty more and a hundred more, snowing down upon the cars around them, upon the crowds on foot. Arnold, opening his window, caught one as it drifted by and saw that it was covered with thumbprints and with words in a foreign language and that it was repeated in Russian.

"They're pages from a petition submitted a few weeks ago to the United Nations Subcommittee on Disarmament, at the approach of its tenth birthday," the consul said. "Ten million signatures were collected throughout neutral Asia and those who couldn't write got their thumbprints down. They said they could have got as many signatures, or thumbprints, as inhabitants, but what they wanted to demonstrate was how fast they could get ten million to commemorate that tenth year. A ban on the bomb, of course. But once they got that stupendous amount of papers to the United Nations and got it noted in the records, they couldn't bear to see it all going up in smoke in the UN incinerators, so they brought them to Hiroshima for today's ceremony. Last night the newspapers announced that helicopters were to scatter them over Nakajima Park to impress you, and there they are." He reached out the window to pick up a sheet of paper lying on the hood. "The signatures, or thumbprints, were collected by the Neutral Asia Confederation of Mothers or some such title. If I remember correctly from the newspaper, it points out the neutrals' natural reluctance to die in a war between two other powers. How does it say . . . ? 'Bombs will fall on other than the belligerents' lands because the belligerents' interests are everywhere, and where the bombs don't fall, fallout will. The fallout from the tests alone has already contaminated Asian soil and Asian rice and the bones of Asian children.' Something like that, if I remember." A sad smile flitted down one side of his mustache. "The ones on my page are from New Delhi," he said, with the sudden brightness of one called upon to be bright, glancing over to see which city Arnold's page was from.

Alma, wedged in between her daughters in the back seat, clicked open and snapped shut the clasp of her purse. "There was something about your speech that I'd like to ask about," she began hesitantly, and he knew that it was hard for her to criticize a speech heard by so many thousands, for it made the platform, in memory, tremble under his feet.

"Yes?" He was both humble and on guard, lamed by his experience and in need of her hand at his elbow.

"You said that the spirit of love, the love that flourished in the midst of the city's disaster—the injured helping the injured—and the love that is evident in the city's rising again from ashes—you said that it's this spirit that will triumph in the world. You said that the rest of the world regarded Hiroshima as a symbol of this spirit."

"That's true, isn't it?" the consul cut in. "I thought it dovetailed so nicely with his explanation of the deterrence theory. The way I got it, if I may paraphrase you," he said apologetically to Arnold, "our missiles prove our love for our fellow men, for with them we preserve the peace. And this spirit of love will triumph over the world as it has in Hiroshima." He cleared his throat as if a lozenge had slipped down into it.

Alma frowned out the window. "They don't mate," she said. "They mate like a flea and an elephant."

The consul laid his brow against the steering wheel, struggling to cough up the lozenge that had now got into his lung. "My dear, I agree with you," he said to her when his voice had a clear passage again. "But it's difficult for me to criticize an immortal speech, the speaker seems so vulnerable." He gestured out at the crowds with their signs and the snow of papers under their feet. "However, when the criticism is made en masse, one can join in, I suppose."

"What was the matter with what he said?" Bernice demanded, her voice like a reed that, carried to a strange climate, can only whisper. "Why is there always something wrong with saying something good?"

The consul started the car again, and as they drove slowly off the grounds, the way cleared for them by traffic policemen, Arnold turned away from the window in an attempt to hide himself from the many persons seeking him out, the ones in the flesh who walked along beside the car, nodding their signs at him, and the ones who were present in their names and their thumbprints on the drifting, trampled papers. Before the hotel, the shuffling throngs were so dense that a narrow path had to be forced for the Elkins family and the consul by two lines of policemen, twenty or so in each line, and when they entered the lobby, the manager at once locked the door.

The consul, watching from their suite the traffic jam below and the crowds pouring in from the park and filling every inch of space in the street before the hotel, suggested that the Elkins family leave the city as soon as possible. He would cancel, he said, the visit of a delegation of complainants scheduled for the afternoon, for by that time the crowds might be rioting, and he would arrange for an Air Force plane to fly the family to the Tokyo Airport. "It appears," he said, and though his brow was dutifully furrowed, the satisfaction that comes of having a prophecy materialize smoothed his lips like a salve, "that your poetry failed to soothe the troubled breast. In fact, your presence seems to be having an effect opposite to the one they intended it to have. Your title is somewhat misleading, you know. The people here seem to ascribe great powers to you. They seem to think you can turn off the missile race like a faucet. Harringer should have sent a congressman, as I said before."

The family was hustled out the back entrance of the hotel and driven by taxi to the airfield. They arrived at noon at the Tokyo International Airport, and Arnold stood in line at the ticket window to pick up their reservations on a plane leaving at two o'clock. With the envelope in his pocket, he wandered out into the waiting room to find the directional sign pointing the way to the restaurant where his wife and daughters had gone.

As he crossed the room, a male voice rattled down from the ceiling, announcing in English the arrival of Nolly Noreen, chosen as Miss Massive Retaliation, Miss MR, in a poll of United States Armed Forces Overseas. At the last syllable, cheering from a hundred male voices rose around Arnold, and from the wall benches surged a battalion of soldiers, the crosscurrents converging upon him and sweeping him along. Not unwillingly, for he was curious, he was swept out onto the edge of the field where a jet plane stood. Gathered before it were civic dignitaries, reporters and photographers, both Japanese and American, and U.S. Army officers. After the entourage of persons—public relations men, secretary, and personal maid, Arnold guessed—had stepped to the ground, Nolly Noreen herself appeared in the doorway and was greeted by a heart-rending moan from the soldiers. Arnold had seen her photographs innumerable times in newspapers and magazines but had not yet got around to attending a motion picture starring her, and so he was not as familiar with her dynamic personality as the young soldiers around him. Nevertheless, the shock of her presence reduced him to a yokel. After ruffling up her pale-gold chrysanthemum hair as if taken by surprise and not quite ready, she began her descent, and the slow jut of her hips under the white silk dress and the light jarring of her breasts as she took each step caused the soldiers to collapse in one another's arms. One soldier fell full length at Arnold's feet but, afraid that he was missing something in that position, he at once jumped up again. And another attempted to climb upon Arnold's back.

A lieutenant general gave her his hand to assist her down, introduced himself and the other officers and the Japanese dignitaries, who bowed. One of the latter group offered her a bouquet of red, white and blue flowers, and as she dipped her face into the bouquet to inhale the fragrance, the cry rose from the welcoming crowd, "One little song! One little song just for us!" A phlegmy voice near Arnold shouted, "Just for the two of us!" and the laughter that followed from the same throat almost blew off Arnold's ear, forcing him to clap his hand over it. From the hundred male voices rose the chant, "Mister, Send Your Missile My Way," which he knew was the title of a popular song, having heard it countless times on the jukebox in the college cafeteria.

Miss Noreen, after handing her bouquet to the lieutenant general and calling for silence by lifting her arms high and fluttering her fingers soothingly down, began to sing in a husky rough-and-tumble voice that, surprisingly, at the end of each verse, jumped an octave and rang out like a frantic dinner bell that feels the hunger of those it summons. The moaning rose around him with each emphatic jolting of her pelvis and each languid twining of her arms toward the audience, and Arnold was able to make out the words of her song only because he had heard them before.

> *Blow my heart to little bits,*
> *Never, never call it quits.*
> *Mister, send your missile my way.*

Amidst the moans and the jumpy voice, he felt a tugging at his sleeve and, glancing down, was surprised to see close at his side Miss Noreen's maid. She was a middle-aged woman, modishly attired in a black silk dress and a black hat that must have belonged at one time to Miss Noreen, for its dipping brim enticed one with a promise of an exciting face underneath. "Give me a cigarette if you've got one," she said, wiggling a finger at his breast pocket. "Miss Noreen smoked my last one."

Quickly he brought out his package, tilting it toward

her. While he was lighting the cigarette for her, she asked him, as if they had been next-door neighbors in the States, "What you doin' in Japan?"

He cleared his throat to rid it of the memory of his speech, of the sweet perfume, and of the acrid match smoke, all combined. "I said a few words at the Memorial," he replied.

"Hey, I didn't get my light!" she complained, and after she had drawn again on her cigarette, she asked him, "You a pastor? You come all the way over here just to bury somebody?"

"The Memorial," he explained, "for the Hiroshima dead."

For a few moments Miss Noreen forced their attention to return to her:

> Conflagrate me, oh please do,
> The man on top's got to be you.
> Mister, send your missile my way.

The woman shoved the straps of her large, black handbag farther up her forearm, preparing to move away from him when the song ended. "They still carry on about that? Might as well set aside a day to cry about everybody in Pompeii."

Nolly Noreen was now reaching farther and singing louder, winding it up.

> That mushroomy cloud is me,
> It's only me in ecstasy.
> Mister, send your missile my way!

And with these last words, the air around him broke into cheers, wolf whistles, stampings, howls. The Army officers, the dignitaries, the cameramen, the reporters, and the entourage, including the maid, closed in around the actress and led her away, and the soldiers closed in behind them, with Arnold following the soldiers.

In the waiting room he caught up with the several soldiers who were unable to push their way out the front entrances and who stood on tiptoe or climbed onto benches. Those who had managed to follow the actress more closely conveyed with their howls to the ones left within the exact moment in which she bent over to enter the car at the curbing. From where he stood in the center of the room, Arnold could see a lavender Cadillac moving off the grounds toward the city, followed by the Army personnel's line of long and shining cars in pastel colors—pink, orange sherbet, sky-blue, spring-green—all with little U.S. flags fluttering at their fenders.

As he was watching the departure, several persons bearing signs began to encircle him. Apologizing to the person he stepped in front of, he slipped through the circle and hurried down the wide corridor toward the restaurant sign he now saw over a far door. When he emerged with his family a few minutes before plane time, the citizens had increased their numbers until they packed the waiting room. They formed a procession behind the family hurrying to the plane, and Arnold, glancing down when the plane was in the air, saw them below, a straggling blot upon the field like a long, black island, like a target in the sea, their tiny signs shaking in the wind.

4

Young Radovan gripped his hand the moment Arnold entered his Triangle office. "I hear that you made quite an impression over there," he cried, fragrant with some spicy lotion that young men use upon their shaven cheeks in the morning. "Had the streets swarming with admirers!" But he was troubled way back in his eyes, as if he, too, had been present and had returned on an earlier plane.

"They weren't admirers," Arnold said. "Since I've done nothing in my short career as Secretary for Humanity to warrant a following. I was a straw for them to grasp." He strode toward the door of his office, hearing himself saying the words he had resolved to say on the trip back. "Get me an appointment with Harringer for today, will you, please?"

Radovan followed him into his office docilely. "As a matter of fact, Harmon phoned a minute ago," he said. "He's upset about the Japanese reaction. Of course, they greeted the Russian Foreign Minister a couple of months ago with a near-riot at the Tokyo Airport—same demands, you know. But your near-riot was the closest yet to the real thing. So he knows about it already."

"He may know about *their* reaction, but he doesn't know about *my* reaction to their reaction," Arnold said.

"He's vitally interested in it, of course," Radovan assured him. "Unfortunately, he's on the farm, in conference with party leaders, working out his campaign. Less than three months left before November fourth. I'd get Eversledge for you but he's out on a destroyer in the Pacific. There's a big covering in color by *Explosion* Magazine of our sonar system. The system is to be called SIS for Sounds in the Sea, one of those easy-to-remember names that won't intimidate the average person when he tries to show some familiarity with our defense system. What happens is that we're able to pick up the position of enemy subs moving in to launch missiles off our coasts. Once we know where they are, we send out a plane to drop an atomic depth charge which, even if it falls several miles away from the sub, will crush in its sides by creating a shock wave in the sea. Anyway, that's where Eversledge is."

"Perhaps I ought to go out to the farm," Arnold persisted, thinning his lips. "It's in Kentucky, isn't it? I could be there in a couple of hours."

"Harmon's paring down interruptions, I'm sure," Radovan replied. "You're a busy man yourself, you know. You're scheduled for the United Nations tomorrow, for the session of the Subcommittee on Disarmament. You'll leave this evening so you'll be ready bright and early in the morning. You can tell me what you have to say about Japan and I'll get copies to both Harmon and Eversledge for you."

Arnold slipped into his pocket the plane tickets that Radovan gave him. "Never mind," he said. "What I have to say to Harmon is the same thing I'm going to say to the Subcommittee. He'll read the speech in the papers."

Alone in his office, he paced back and forth, his plea forming in longhand notes before his eyes, superimposing itself upon the pages of the Hiroshima speech. He would convey the message from the Japanese people, which, translated into the language of negotiation, meant that each proposal presented to the Subcommittee must be considered as if it were a lifeline to a drowning man. The fibers were not to be examined for possible unraveling, and the name and the nationality of whoever threw the line were not to be asked. As he paced, he fingered the page of thumbprints from Djakarta that he had folded up and placed in his coat pocket as he sat in the consul's car.

The plane that carried the Elkins family and forty-six other passengers to New York arrived at the airport a few minutes after a private plane, also from Washington, D.C. The Elkins family skirted a group of newsmen and photographers surrounding a man in a Homburg, who disengaged himself from the group and, with his attaché at his heels, strode toward a white Chrysler in whose driver's seat sat a uniformed chauffeur.

Arnold, cramping himself and his family inside a taxi for the ride to the hotel that Radovan had chosen for them, said, his voice clear as a bell within the dingy interior, "This is the way I like it."

Alma tugged her skirt from under Becky. "Before Japan I didn't mind," she said.

"Why not after?" he asked. "Since Japan I see what the 'humanity' means in the title they gave me."

"It seemed all right when Radovan explained it," she went on. "No style, no conspicuous comfort. But now I think there's something wrong with it. Nobody here at home cares whether you come or go, and maybe it's because you lack the kind of weight you get in a car like that," nodding toward the dignitary's car as it passed them.

In the lobby of the Great Midtown Hotel, a small place in a row of small hotels, sat elderly men with the aspect of transients at last come to roost among the comforts of home, which were the TV set and the many sofas. The ascent in the creaking elevator had the same effect upon Arnold as the ride in the taxi. He felt his potential stirring in his chest. In spite of their dour faces, he guessed that his family was harboring the same hope for him, for when the bellboy unlocked the door of their room and a large, penny-colored cockroach scuttled limpingly across the floor, he heard no cry of alarm, no muttered complaint.

The delegate who called to escort Arnold to the United Nations headquarters was Cameron Corby, an ex-senator from California, who, upon his defeat at the polls four years before, had been immediately appointed as a delegate by Harringer. The nation, the President had told the press, could not afford to waste the capabilities of the man. He waited for Arnold in the lobby, a large man whose vitality seemed to increase his circumference, impelling others to give him room to breathe. Arnold, as they went out the door together, recollected the drawings in the story of the big-faced wind that blew with all his might but could not blow the jacket off the spindly man.

On the sidewalk before the hotel a crowd had gathered, and he saw, protruding from among the figures, the head of a small horse with largish ears. Around its neck hung a garland of red roses.

"I brought along an ass for you to ride to the UN," Corby explained. "I figured that the man who had the courage to take over that title they gave you would certainly have the courage to carry it through." He clasped his hands together to make a stirrup. "May I help you mount?"

Arnold shook his head. It had always seemed to him that the victim of a practical joke did not salvage his dignity by laughing at himself but rather by impressing a tolerant smile upon his tormentor, and this he did to Corby. "Overemphasis sometimes takes us farther away from the point," he said.

"Come along in my car, then." Corby put his hand on Arnold's back to steer him toward the longest car that Arnold had ever seen, a dark-red car with six broad strips of chromium along the sides and six headlights recessed within a huge chromium mouth. "Though I think the overemphasizing has already been done by whoever dreamed you up. If you will forgive me, your post has Christlike connotations. It makes the rest of us seem less than we ought to be."

At the delegates' entrance, Corby took his elbow and escorted him inside the building, breasting the tide of history with a broad chest.

"You've got to have a sense of humor around here," Corby said, as if he sensed Arnold's hurt and desired to make amends. "If you took everything seriously you wouldn't last a day. All proposals are presented with such sincerity you'd be weeping all the salt out of your body if you believed everybody. They'd have to install salt tablets by the drinking fountains."

In the committee room, Arnold was introduced to the delegates. All of them wished him success in his cabinet post, all except the delegate from India, a frail young woman in a saffron sari. "If, as Mr. Corby has said, your aim as Secretary for Humanity is to lift from the heart of humanity the fear of the bomb, then I do not wish for your success," she said.

Corby laughed with chesty kindliness. "You've got some word confused with another."

"No." She was not offended by Corby's comment; it amused her almost as much as it amused Corby himself. "No," she repeated. "I know the meaning of the word *fear*. And I am afraid it is just the fear you are worried about. There is an admonition made famous by one of your presidents that is still applied on occasion by lesser statesmen in their speeches. It goes, 'The only thing we have to fear is fear itself.' I am of the opinion that this belief has become deeply rooted in your nation's consciousness, and that, I think, is extremely unfortunate. You believe that to be afraid of anything is to be cowardly, even if the anything is the incineration of your entire population in a nuclear war. The trouble is that you do not fear the nuclear war, you fear the fear of it. Therefore, if Mr. Elkins is to lift the fear from your hearts, I do not wish him success." She wound her colorful, silken way among the dark-suited delegates and sat down at her designated place at the table.

Corby, drawing in his chair, remarked, "The trouble with her is that she takes everything you say literally. She always gets me into arguments over the meaning of what I'm saying. It's the language barrier. She doesn't know our idiom and I don't know hers. Imagine her thinking we want everybody to welcome a nuclear war with open arms."

He ran his fingers through his bouncy black-and-gray hair. "You see what I mean when I say you've got to have a sense of humor?"

"This is the largest subcommittee I could imagine," Arnold commented, seating himself at Corby's side.

Up rose the chairman, a portly Britisher with heavy spectacles, and called the meeting to order. He read the resolution passed many years before by the General Assembly, creating the Subcommittee and outlining its purpose, and then, with a smile of satisfaction, announced that this day's session marked its tenth year. Removing his spectacles, smoothing his eyebrows with a small, plump hand, he began a résumé of the Subcommittee's years of parley. It was agreed among them, he said, that no country would emerge victorious in the event of nuclear war. In the space of three days, he said, the world could be destroyed. The products of man's intelligence through the long centuries, from the artifacts of the paleolithic period to the space rockets to the moon, all destroyed. The tangible objects created by man from the materials of the earth, from water, air and fire, from wood and stone and metal, from minerals and chemicals, all destroyed. The written word, the composers' notes, the equations of science, lost forever. The only alternative to this catastrophe, he said, was disarmament. "However," he said, "the ways to achieve disarmament are not yet agreed upon."

Arnold, glancing around while the chairman spoke, found the other delegates also glancing around or conversing *sotto voce* or flicking through their papers or gazing out into space with their fingers draped at their temples. The chairman's voice was not demanding of attention. It had the monotony of garden shears at work, clipping a hedge down to a certain height under the windows of the conference room.

Hooking on his glasses again, the chairman reminded them of the Subcommittee's growth. In the beginning, five delegates had comprised it and now there were nineteen. The number of nuclear nations was growing, and the Subcommittee right along with it, for more delegates were required to tackle a more complicated problem. The delegate from China, he said, was the most recently welcomed, his country, in an extraordinary situation, having attained the roster of nuclear nations *before* it attained the roster of the United Nations. For a time, he said, the Soviet Union had withdrawn from the Subcommittee and, for a time, the United States had withdrawn, but both had reinstated themselves because of the need for the Subcommittee. And he smiled a thin, smug smile with his nostrils, the smile of a lover or a parent who is returned to.

"If we are in constant deadlock," he said, "it is not because we will it that way. Every proposal has been given, in its time, profound consideration. Every delegate has examined his conscience, and rejections have been based, not upon whim or stubbornness, false pride or ignorance, but upon each delegate's anxious desire to safeguard the citizens of his own country, their lives, their sacred honor, their social system. And this responsibility calls for and receives the highest logic, the deepest passion. Indeed," he said, "it is from this concern for one's own people that there will come an age of peace based upon iron-clad guarantees of peace." Shuffling his papers together, lifting his face, animated by good will, he concluded, "We can therefore take heart from the fact that this Subcommittee exists still, that in spite of seemingly insoluble differences, in spite of increasing difficulties that follow upon the development of newer, more destructive weapons and upon the inclusion of further nations in the family of nuclear nations, this Subcommittee continues to function. No catastrophic war has put an end to this Subcommittee. For ten years its members have sat down together, and with God's help we will sit down together for another ten years and more. We have little to despair about and much to rejoice in." The chairman sat down, the other delegates shifted in their chairs, and one removed his glasses and massaged the bridge of his nose.

"An anniversary is always a shot in the arm," Corby said. "But even a shot in the arm doesn't restore life. Some of these fellows, notably the Russians, are what you might call dead, they're so heavily doped with distrust."

To Arnold, the air of the room had a peculiar sealed quality, though the ceiling was spaciously high, and the delegates appeared small in the architectural scheme of the chamber, and the place rustled with each delegate's cognizance of the critical times and the part that he played in making the times more or less so. "I don't quite see the origins of his optimism," he said.

Corby scrutinized him closely. "You're not going to accomplish anything without optimism. Suppose whenever I got up to speak, I pulled a long, pessimistic face. The opposition would imagine there's a weak spot somewhere, a cancer somewhere, and all they've got to do is aggravate the invalid and wait for his demise. Anybody, any nation that's ever accomplished anything, has been optimistic about results. It's breath in the body."

Arnold smiled a lopsided, humorless smile. "In the meantime," he said, "back at the H-bomb factory . . ."

Corby's manner changed. The amiability left his blue eyes. "I meant to ask you for a copy of your speech that you intend to deliver here," he said. "I want to look it over and check on time and applicability and delete statements that might, unwittingly, of course, undermine our position."

Arnold tapped his temple. "I intend to deliver it extemporaneously," he said. "When I've given deep thought to any subject I'm able to lecture on that subject with only a few notes. The notes that I do have," he said, rummaging through his pockets and bringing up four white filing cards, "are indecipherable to anyone but myself."

Frowning, Corby glanced at the cryptic notes as another delegate rose to speak. "We should have got together sooner about this," he said hastily. "Suppose we go over your notes this evening? I've been on this Subcommittee for four years now and nobody's had cause for complaint. I'm sure Harringer will respect my desire to exercise caution in this case." He lifted his bluntly handsome profile toward the speaker.

The delegate from the Soviet Union was a slender fellow with black hair flapping over his brow. His high cheekbones were like ramparts for his eyes. "When I was attached to the Soviet Embassy in Washington, D.C.," he began, "I would pick up a newspaper in the morning and I would read in the headlines: 'U.S. Tells Russia to Put Up or Shut Up.' This at first was a puzzle to me. What does one put up? And if one cannot put up, why must one shut up? It seemed to me that if one does not put up then one does the opposite of shut up, one talks it out with the other to see if both can put up. But since those early days of my career, I have learned that in spite of its unreasonableness it is a national motto, it is a philosophy peculiar to the United States. And do you know why? Because they don't want to talk anything over unless, before you begin, you agree to agree with them."

Corby, amiable again, ducked his head toward Arnold. "They're always heavy on the sarcasm," he said. "They like it as much as they like sour cream, but does it solve anything?"

Without once consulting the papers before him, the

Soviet delegate listed the occasions that the U.S. had demonstrated its rigidity, taking thirty minutes for this before continuing on: "They have dug pits and traps for this Subcomittee ever since its inception, but the greatest stumbling block they have put in its path is their insistence upon their package deal. Always they insist upon this package deal. We will not, they say, talk over a ban of nuclear bomb testing unless we can, at the same time, talk over a thousand and one other items. And what are these other items? Each of them requires years of negotiations. But, they say, unless we solve these other problems, also and at the same time, we cannot be sure that you, the Soviet Union, will observe the testing ban. The solution of these other items will serve, they say, as the guarantee. A tremendously complex situation and they make it sound so simple. Everything in one package, like the TV dinners you buy in the market." He straightened his papers with a stern hand. "So when I read in the newspapers this morning, as I drank my coffee, that this session marks the tenth year of this Subcommittee and that the U.S. delegate, Cam Corby, is prepared to tell the USSR delegate to put up or shut up, I knew, of course, what to expect today. We will adjourn today in the same deadlock. But because it is an anniversary, I wish to make a prediction. I predict that if a nuclear war erupts, as a result of the refusal of the United States to take the first step with us toward disarmament, that the last words the citizens of that country will utter will be 'Put up or shut up!'—a cry which they will imagine is their rallying cry but which will be, instead, their epitaph."

Corby rose, bowed his head to wait for the air to clear itself of the voice of the previous speaker, then pointed his chin at the Soviet delegate, who was conferring with his aide as if no one else had risen. "We have a dread of loopholes," he began. "The peoples of the free world, who have won their freedom by blood and by toil, have a dread in their hearts of the loophole through which tyranny enters. The common experience of every man teaches us that the negotiator who desires to eliminate from the contract the stipulations that bind him is not all that he claims to be. Only the man, only the nation, that is willing to include, yes, a thousand and one stipulations, is the nation, is the man, that we can trust." He lowered his head and appeared to be waiting for applause to die down. "We are attempting here," he said, "to negotiate with a nation not unsullied by its past, a nation in whose ledger of history are listed its crimes against humanity. And we say to that nation: First, demonstrate your good intentions by discussing your captive neighbors, the little nations that cower in dread along your borders, under the heels of your puppet rulers. Then we will go on from there and discuss other stipulations, and for each stipulation we will take as much time as we deem necessary. We will demand as many guarantees as we deem necessary, for we know your past full well." Half an hour went by with his enumeration of some of the acts of deception practiced by the Soviet Union. When he had finished with his task, his voice was heavy-laden. "Our package disarmament plan is basic to our free world's defense," he concluded. "And we will not be satisfied with less, as we have never in our history been satisfied with less than the best in every aspect of our national existence. To ask us to sacrifice even one small safeguard is to reveal an abysmal ignorance of the dynamics of our democracy. We are a democracy by reason of our desire never to be satisfied with partial measures, with second best. The package proposal has become for us a symbol of the democracy that we are defending with it."

Arnold, in the moment before Corby sat down, reached

over and with his index finger drew toward him the few white filing cards which bore the notations for his speech. So desirous was he of speaking to the Subcommittee now that he had heard these first speeches, that he cleared his throat as if he had already been introduced, with one hand gripped the edge of the table and with the other repossessed his cards by laying it flat upon them. They had disagreed for a decade in this committee and was it something to commemorate? He felt that the shame upon them all was so great that each one, as he spoke, ought to put up his arms across his face. While they counted up each other's sins, they joined together in contaminating the earth and in preparing for its end. The opening sentence was on his tongue: *I have been told to be optimistic, but there is no time left.*

The chairman recognized the delegate from Sweden, who rose at Arnold's right, giving him a start. With a genial, lightweight voice, the delegate congratulated the Subcommittee on its decade of service to humanity. "We are not the few delegates who gathered together that first day," he said. "Since that day the problem confronting the Subcommittee has grown from a simple algebraic equation to an astrophysical one, and the Subcommittee has kept pace with it. For now, some of those among the lesser nations, the nonnuclear nations, have grown up and have taken their places around the table. They, too, possess the hydrogen bomb." Placing his fingertips on the table, he continued: "We recall that in 1958 the United Nations Political Committee placed itself on record as 'recognizing that a danger existed that an increase of the number of states possessing nuclear weapons may occur, aggravating international tensions and the difficulty of maintaining world peace, and thus rendering more difficult the attainment of general disarmament.' Some among that committee called for a most unrealistic proposal that would have requested the nuclear powers, three at that time, to refrain from transferring nuclear weapons to nonnuclear allies and would have requested the nonnuclear nations to refrain from producing nuclear weapons. Fortunately, the proposal was quashed in embryo. The most its proponents achieved was that committee's placing itself on record as recognizing the danger." He consulted the backs of his hands. "The point I desire to make is that a small nation's attainment of maturity through possession of nuclear weapons is, indeed, worth the risks involved. Instead of a few paternal nations and many small, immature nations, we now have several powerful nations and others well on their way to becoming so. And what is so satisfactory about it—the size of the nation does not matter, its geographical size, the size of its treasury, and so forth. For the smallest nation is as mighty as the mightiest. The nuclear bomb is the great equalizer." After granting the members a few moments of silence in which to appreciate the aphorism he had coined, he continued: "It is evident to us that the entire world must be thankful that the possession of nuclear weapons is passing from the hands of the few to the hands of the many, for it is those nations now on the road to becoming nuclear nations and those who have only recently entered the camp of nuclear nations who demand not only a thousand and one guarantees, but twice that many, double locks and triple locks. For they will not give up so soon what they have achieved or are, at last, achieving. And it may well be that the Political Committee's warning of a world in which the probability of war by accident or war by design would increase with the spread of nuclear technology will prove to be pessimistically wrong. For it is the newer nuclear nation's insistence upon ironclad guarantees, it is this insistence that will insure an ironclad peace for the peoples of the world."

When the Swedish delegate had seated himself, the chairman dismissed the Subcommittee, requesting the members to return at two o'clock that afternoon.

"But they've only begun, or not even that," Arnold complained.

"The eternal verities always chop up these sessions. It's time for lunch," Corby said, gathering his papers into his attaché case.

As they went along the corridor to the restaurant for delegates, Arnold asked, "What did the committee do about the petition from Asia? When I was in Japan, the pages of the petition were dropped from helicopters upon the mourners leaving the park. In my address I intend to mention the incident."

Corby took his elbow to hurry him around a cluster of diplomats. "We acknowledged its receipt," he said. "What more do you want? Do you know what it called for? Treason. It called upon the delegates to the Subcommittee to ban nuclear weapons regardless of censure or punishment from their governments, called upon them to urge all nuclear workers—scientists, engineers, everyone—to cease their work and to prefer starvation and even execution rather than a prosperity based upon the suffering and extinction of humanity. It sounded," he said, "most impressively urgent, like a last resort sort of thing, and among the first signers were the President of Indonesia, government officials in India, in Cambodia, the works. But nobody on the committee was in a treasonable mood and so it was doomed to failure. A naïve appeal from men you would expect to be wiser."

Other delegates were converging on the restaurant, and not until Arnold was almost in the doorway did he see the old man standing to one side of it, a man taller than himself, gaunt, sallow, with twigs of gray hair growing in several directions above his broad brow.

"Karl Flugeltaube," whispered Corby in Arnold's ear. "He's completely gone, you'll see." Smiling largely, he clapped his hand on the old man's shoulder to introduce him to Arnold, but even before the names had left Corby's mouth, Arnold was clasping the extended hand in both of his, so eager and so honored was he to meet the man called the century's greatest humanitarian. Flugeltaube appeared as impressed by Arnold as Arnold was by him, for the old man pumped his hand, and his sunken green eyes glimmered in his large, bony face.

"Be our guest," said Corby, and the old man, weightless as a leaf from hunger, was blown inside on Corby's hospitable breath. The three sat down at a small table covered by a snow-white cloth, and the waiter hastened to place a menu before each one.

"Ah, Secretary for Humanity. That is a beautiful title," said Flugeltaube, clasping his hands together on the cloth and gazing at Arnold. Wasn't he past ninety? thought Arnold. Over his skin was a brown mottling, as on decaying fruit, and at his temples and on his hands rose swollen sprays of blue veins.

"Are you on vacation from your hospital in the Amazon jungle?" Arnold asked.

Flugeltaube ordered tea, toast and honey, and a bunch of grapes. "I have been at the United Nations for six years," he replied.

"But I seem to recall," said Arnold, "that you once said that you would never leave the Amazon Valley, that you felt that there, ministering to the natives, your skill as a physician was utilized for the greatest good."

The doctor smiled nostalgically. "When I ventured into

the Brazilian jungle, set up my hospital there and healed the jungle Indians of their indigenous diseases, my face was on the covers of the most popular magazines of all countries and in the Sunday supplements. They called me the greatest humanitarian of the century. Artists came into the jungle to study me from all angles in order to carve in stone the likeness of my magnificent head. Writers interviewed me, and a novel was written about me, the genius son of a famous German philosopher and a famous English poetess, daughter of a Lord, who met in the reading rooms of the British Museum, a son who became physician and philosopher and who left the world of culture and enlightenment to assist the benighted natives of Brazil. All very true, and it became a best seller. Nurses came to me from all parts of the world, traveled on pittances, endured privations to come and assist me. Kings and princes sailed up the Amazon to visit me, and the wealthy of the world sent their philanthropic checks. For fifty years I was famous. They never tired of me. Why, the year before I left, on the fiftieth year of my hospital, we received fourteen grants from as many foundations, and the *Illustrated London News*, the French *Scientific Bulletin*, your weekly picture magazine *Explosion*, were but a few among many periodicals relating my history again. The last magazine ran twelve full-page colored photographs of everything—the jungle, the nurses, the hospital, the patients, and several of myself, reading, playing the violin, holding the hand of an old native woman dying." He thanked the waiter, poured tea into his cup. "But now I am forgotten as completely as if I had died disgraced six years ago."

Corby unfolded his napkin. "I advise you to begin your salad," he said to Arnold. "There's an afternoon session, you know."

The old doctor sipped his tea. "Since I have established

residence, so to speak, at the United Nations, in order to convince the delegates of the necessity to accept my plan to save the world, those editors who before had sung my praises now fail to recognize me. I have begged for publicity, for a page or two of their magazines so that I might state my belief, but they consider me as devoid of reason as an old man with a case of syphilitic paresis." He picked up a triangle of toast, spread honey on it. "It does seem odd to me," he said, "that when I saved but two hundred lives a year they compared me with Christ, but now when I wish to save the lives of millions"—and he shrugged a lonely shoulder—"they deny my existence."

Corby laid down his soup spoon and wiped his mouth with a corner of his large white napkin. "If I remember correctly," he said, "you took pride, formerly, in your aloofness from politics. It may be that they decline to see you because you are now as soiled as the rest of us."

Flugeltaube gazed at Corby uncomprehendingly. "I am echoing no voice save the one that comes from my heart," he said.

Corby lifted judicious eyebrows. "What you are envisioning is Utopia and it's just the kind of scheme the enemy could use, because somewhere along the line, most likely at the beginning, they'd begin their termiting of the whole structure. Utopias fall harder and sooner than anything else, you know." And glancing sideways at Arnold's plate, "Again, I advise you to eat."

The old man spooned more honey on his toast, and some that dripped over the side he caught on his spoon and carried to his mouth. "When I called upon the Soviet delegate, he said that he was in agreement with the disarmament aspect of my proposal but disagreed with the rest of it, the answer to what to do with the resources that disarmament will free. The Soviet Union, he told me, would

not countenance United Nations' control of or inter-
ference in its economic affairs. On parting with me, he
said that only when communism covers the earth will there
be the Utopia I call for, and I presume it is your belief that
capitalism over all the earth is the only condition for
Utopia. No matter," he sighed. "When it comes it will
come as itself, nothing else can come in the guise of it.
And it will come because it must, because humanity can't
live much longer without it. The patient requires it to survive." He leaned toward Arnold and a breeze from somewhere stirred softly the upstanding twigs of hair. "I shall
be happy," he said, "to explain my plan to you in detail.
We could go into the reading room. The afternoon session will, no doubt, be a continuation of the self-righteous
lectures of the morning. They are commemorating the
tenth year as if they had accomplished something by a
mystic effect of numbers."

Since he had no hope of delivering his speech that day
and since he was grateful for an afternoon in the company
of Karl Flugeltaube, Arnold accepted the invitation. When
lunch was over and he parted from Corby in the corridor,
he noted with a small pang of humiliation that the
delegate was in no way troubled by the parting. In fact, his
stride down the corridor away from them was one of accomplishment. In leaving Arnold with Flugeltaube, he
had done a favor for them both, bringing them together
so that they could delight in each other's odd company in
a corner of their own.

With a large, comforting hand the old man took Arnold's elbow and steered him down corridors, into a public
reading room, and over to a couch by a window where
venetian blinds filtered the hot sun glaring down upon
the city. From his old, stained, leather portfolio he took
out the papers that had made it bulge and placed the pile

between them on the couch.

"That was quite a reception they gave you in Japan," the old man said. "The number and size of demonstrations continue to increase throughout the world. In England, you may have heard, thirty thousand persons marched at Eastertime from the Aldermaston Atomic Research Establishment to Trafalgar Square in London, a distance of fifty miles. In Paris, only last Sunday, seventeen thousand women in black marched through the streets to protest French bomb tests in North Africa, in spite of a ban upon such demonstrations. And in Africa, nine thousand persons traveled from almost every country of that continent to the Sahara Desert, where the tests are in progress. However, in the Soviet Union and the United States, protest seems to be on a minor scale. Can you explain the atypical behavior in this country?"

"As far as I can see," Arnold replied, "nobody believes that the bombs will fall. Everyone in the Defense Department subscribes to the theory that the more weapons and the bigger weapons we have, the less chance there is of war. This theory is accepted by the public."

The old man took from his coat pocket a paper napkin and wiped his eyes. "The earth," he said, "is covered with ICBM bases, pock-marked with them as with a disease symptom, but they don't believe that death can follow."

Arnold put his finger on the top folder of the pile. "What's your remedy?" he asked.

"Not mine alone," the doctor replied. "This is the work of men and women who are authorities in their fields and who, through correspondence and conferences, evolved the plan together. They are citizens of many nations, including the United States and the Soviet Union. Economists, agronomists, biologists, nutritionists, engineers, medical researchers, educators, social scientists.

Separately and together they examined humanity's needs, and oh! what tremendous needs! When this was done, they worked out the ways and means to fill the needs. They took the expenditure of all nations engaged in the production of weapons, the total expenditure since the end of the last World War, and broke it down, this tremendous total, into projects that would have been possible had the treasure gone into the research and development of all things beneficial to humanity. If it had been so used, we would now be living in the midst of the most amazing epoch. Arid lands springing into bloom over all the earth, great dams rising on the rivers. And against the diseases that plague humanity and, of course, against the conditions that produce the diseases of the body and the soul, ah, the advances!" He massaged his thigh with his large, seemingly weightless hand. "You said something?"

"I'm listening," Arnold replied. "I said nothing."

Flugeltaube placed a sheaf of papers in Arnold's lap. "What we must do is persuade the United Nations to make this conversion compulsory. The difficulty we encounter is each nation's obsession with working out its own destiny. Unfortunately, that destiny appears to be a collective end of all their destinies." He tapped the papers with his knuckles. "They've got it figured out in detail, if you care to see. For example, the two hundred and fifty million dollars for an ICBM base would do wonders—and they detail these wonders—for the backward agricultural methods of . . . What country does it say there?" he asked, bending over the small type. "Ah, when I think of the billions the world spent last year for war preparation, for it is difficult for me to think of the grand total of the years, when I think of that monstrous fraction of the total and then see before my eyes the hungry faces of India, of Pakistan, the sick and illiterate faces one finds everywhere, the faces of men who die of the cold in the great cities of the world . . . Can you find the name of that country?" he asked, his old eyes still seeking, his finger wandering over the page.

"That grand total is for all weapons, you say?" Arnold asked.

"The proposal calls for total disarmament, if that's what you're asking," Flugeltaube replied. "When the absurdity of nuclear war becomes apparent to the extent that all nations disarm themselves of these weapons, it follows as a natural law that all other methods of war become absurd. The absurdity of the instruments of man's inhumanity increases with the decrease in their number. As you lop off one, the next, though less massive, becomes as absurd as the one that went before—until the last rifle in the empty arsenal is absurd."

Arnold shook his head. "But I recall the resolution for total disarmament approved in 1959 by all the nations then in the United Nations. It came to nothing. It was too big."

"On the contrary, it was too little," Flugeltaube replied. "When something is taken away, something else must be put in its place. When the means for mass death is removed, it follows, does it not, that the means for life must take its place. This they failed to see." Again he glanced at Arnold as if encouraging him to interrupt.

"Go on, please," Arnold told him.

The old man combed out with his index finger one straggly side of his gray mustache. "Are you to speak before the Subcommittee?" he asked.

"Corby is to confer with me this evening about my speech," Arnold replied.

"What did you have in mind to say?" Flugeltaube asked.

Arnold, sitting with the papers in his lap, recalled the speech he had intended to make, that urgent plea for an acceptance of any and all lifelines, and although it had seemed that morning an imperative proposal, a proposal of great substance, it now seemed meager.

Unable to wait for an answer, Flugeltaube went on, "Would you consider pleading for an adoption of this plan?"

"Corby wouldn't permit it," Arnold replied.

Draping his hand over his mustache, the old man said through his fingers, "What do you think of getting his approval for a congratulatory statement to the Subcommittee and then delivering a different speech?"

"I'd lose my job," Arnold said.

"Ah, but think of the reverberations!" the old man cried. "Even if Corby denied, afterward, that you spoke for the United States, the very fact of your calling for conversion would reveal the beginnings of a schism in Washington and lead the delegates of other nations toward receptivity. Did you say something?" he asked again, in a hoarse whisper.

"I may have said 'yes' without knowing that I said it," Arnold replied.

The old man sighed with delight, a billowy sigh in several stages. "It will be spectacular," he said. "The Secretary for Humanity acting on his own."

Groups on tour of the United Nations, led by pretty girls in uniform, peered at intervals into the reading room as they went along the corridor to more vital rooms, where history was enacted. All afternoon Arnold read the details of Flugeltaube's proposal. The glare disappeared from the window and the old man got up and stood for a long time peering out between the slats of the venetian blind, his hands clasped behind him. At five o'clock, Flugeltaube returned the papers to his portfolio, and the two men went out to board a bus.

As they clung to the horizontal bar above their heads to

avoid being pitched against the other passengers in the aisle, Flugeltaube spoke into Arnold's ear. "My evenings are spent in pursuit of funds to sustain myself," he said. "I refuse to accept even a small part of the money that is sent to me by persons who desire to support me while I support the plan at the UN. Instead, I send the money to Hiroshima, to the Home for Defective Children. There seems to be a significant percent of microcephaly among children exposed to the bomb *in utero,* and the genetic damage done to the bomb survivors is showing up now among their children. More microcephaly and a variety of skeletal, visceral, and nervous system abnormalities. This particular home cares for the first, the microcephalics. They seem to be a commentary on the perversion of man's intellect, do they not?" He sighed. "Tonight, I shall be given a free meal by the proprietor of a small café on 129th Street. Other nights, I have other friends, and some even donate to the home when the day's profits permit it."

They shook hands in farewell, and the old man pushed past the cluster of passengers at the exit and leaped with eccentric agility down the steps, overcompensating after fifty years in the jungle for the ineptness that was thrust upon him by the clanging and snapping vehicles of the city.

Arnold's family was waiting for him in the hotel room, fanning themselves in the warm evening with fans made of magazine pages. They had watched the afternoon proceedings of the Disarmament Subcommittee, they told him, and had wondered at his absence. They had expected him, they said, to make his speech. Arnold sat down on the edge of the bed, and Becky fanned his head.

"They've adjourned until September," Alma told him. "They adjourned in order to consider exhaustively a major alteration in the United States' proposal for conventional weapons disarmament. Last month, the Soviet Union agreed to what the U.S. asked for, after almost three years, but today Corby withdrew the proposal, explaining that the withdrawal was necessitated by an evolving situation, and then the Soviet delegate jumped to his feet and accused the U.S. of insincerity to begin with in advancing the proposal. Then the woman delegate from India said that since it had taken this long to make a dent in conventional weapons and the dent wasn't made yet and the conventional is only a minor appendage of the nuclear weapons system, it will take one hundred years for a dent to be made in the nuclear system. And she said that the chairman's birthday wish for longevity was not enough to keep the Subcommittee or the rest of the world alive that long. She predicted that the last session of the Subcommittee would be held, perhaps soon, in the shelter being constructed for delegates in the basement and that it would be a most disorderly session but also the most conclusive. She was eloquent and impassioned; you should have heard her."

"They adjourn too often," Becky said. "They ought to stay in that room year in and year out, sleep on the floor and the table and have sandwiches and coffee brought in. Nobody ought to be permitted to leave."

Arnold bent his head to rub his forehead cruelly, as if his forehead were rusty iron and he was cleaning it with a wire brush. Becky, slowing down the fan to watch him, touched him with the edge of it and apologized. In the anxious silence around him, he dropped his hand. "My head aches," he explained. "All afternoon I was preparing the speech I had hoped to be able to make tomorrow." He told them of his meeting with Flugeltaube and of the proposal that he had examined and of his promise to the old man to promote that proposal. "This will be a blow to him," he said, rising.

They walked out into the street to find a restaurant and saw along the way, among the myriad of other signs, the yellow fluorescent arrows that pointed to fallout shelters already existing in the basements of the buildings or accessible through the basements. One block of ancient hotels was half demolished. The giant wrecking ball was still, its work done for the day, and the rooms that it had broken open were exposed high in the air, their painted walls, their dark and moldy wallpaper walls, their interior doors to nowhere exposed. And it seemed to Arnold that the privacy of all past tenants, whoever had lived in those rooms, was violated, though they might be now on the other edge of the country or dead for twenty years. A large sign erected above the fence that surrounded the demolition explained that a public shelter to accommodate seven thousand persons was to be constructed on the site by the Capperwell & Blaggett Corporation; and following this large-lettered information was a list of firms equipping the shelter, including a plumbing firm, a foam rubber firm, a plastics firm. The family dined at a small restaurant where red lipstick flecked the rims of the water glasses and an insect resembling an earwig floated in Bernice's bowl of vegetable soup. Arnold calmed their stomachs with the comment, "Of all the tragic decisions in the world today, this is the least tragic," and they returned to their hotel.

On their way through the lobby their attention was caught by the TV screen, and over the heads of the elderly guests seated on the sofas, they watched a boy of ten huddling against a wall, crying piteously. The screen shook with the sobs of the boy. The image of the boy receded as the camera took in more of the wall, revealing a sign above his head reading: BE CALM AND COURTEOUS WHILE

88

YOU ARE IN THIS SHELTER. In the next instant, his face, over which was spreading an extreme joy, occupied the entire screen. A black-and-white terrier was revealed as the cause of his joy, a dog carried in the arms of another boy who approached in a searching manner. The dog then leaped into the arms of the boy huddled by the wall, and at that moment a blast rocked the screen and the lobby. The boy, a tender smile upon his tear-stained face, the dog clasped in his arms, lifted his eyes toward the source of the blast, above. A throng of people, kits in hand, strode across the screen, hiding him from view, and when they had grown dense enough to serve as a background, the large white words

For the Stray that May Come Your Way
Put a Can of BLUE CHAMP *into Your Kit*
NOW

were superimposed upon the throng.

Arnold felt a tapping at his shoulder and, turning, found Karl Flugeltaube behind him, smiling with the pleasure of seeing him again.

"Is this your hotel?" Arnold asked. "Or did you come to see me?"

"This is my hotel," Flugeltaube explained, taking his flat wallet from his pocket and unfolding it to show them six single dollar bills. "And happily, this evening I managed to collect enough to pay for the half a week that is owing. The fry cook at the café contributed three dollars, the waitress two dollars, and a customer next to me at the counter another dollar. I explained to them about my rent." He slipped the wallet into his trouser pocket and with the bills in his hand turned toward the clerk at the desk.

Arnold asked the clerk for the keys to the rooms occu-

pied by his family, and along with the keys was handed a
telegram. Unfolding it, he saw that Radovan was the
sender and that it called upon him to return to Washington in the morning. He glanced at Flugeltaube who
was accepting the receipt for the rent. "My friend," he said,
"obviously you haven't heard that the Subcommittee has
adjourned. And this telegram is from my assistant, calling
me home."

The old doctor leaned on Arnold as they walked the
few steps to the elevator, his bones heavy as lead. "After so
many years of laboring in vain at the UN, you were the
answer to my prayers," he said. "It would have been the
golden apple on the barren tree. A man in your post speaking on his own and speaking for humanity would have laid
bare their narrow, national little souls. But now tomorrow
will be like every other day."

They entered the elevator and Flugeltaube rode with
them to the sixth floor, the last. At the door of the room
before their rooms, he halted and inserted his key in the
lock. Pleading weariness, he declined to visit with them
and bade them good night. For several minutes after they
had entered their room, Arnold and his wife heard him
still fumbling at his lock.

The blind had been down all day against the sun, and
when the lights were out, Arnold, before climbing into
bed beside his wife, pulled up the blind to permit the night
air to enter and freshen the room. A dancing, jittery sea of
colors flowed down into the window. In the space of one
minute the color in the room changed countless times, and
Arnold, gazing up at the towers, saw among the closest
signs one in red and yellow, instructing him to

BE HUMANE
TAKE A STRAY INTO THE SHELTER

and when these words disappeared,

BLUE CHAMP

blossomed forth in blue letters twelve feet tall. With his hands gripping the sill, he watched the sign repeat itself again and again, its colors bathing his lifted face.

Arnold swung a chair up to his assistant's desk, straddled it, and pointed to the telephone a few inches away from Radovan's hand. "Get me Harringer on his farm," he said. "He'll be glad you interrupted his campaign conference."

"Eversledge is back," Radovan told him.

"Not Eversledge."

Radovan frowned, troubled, as one who hears a friend speak against another friend. "What have you got against James?"

"Only that he won't appreciate it," Arnold said, and knowing that he would be compelled to explain Flugel-taube's plan to Radovan before he would be permitted to explain it to Eversledge, and to Eversledge before Harringer, he slapped his brief case on the desk and unzipped it with an executive's positive, impatient fingers. "I have here," he said, "some notes I copied from the portfolio of a gentleman I met at the United Nations. He and his organization have worked out in minute detail a plan for an international . . ."

"Ah, yes," said Radovan. "There was an item about him on the TV news this morning."

"Flugeltaube?" asked Arnold, glancing up in surprise.

"He died," Radovan said, holding out his hand for the notes that Arnold was passing to him. "Collapsed of a heart attack early this morning while he was dressing in his hotel room. They said that he was senile in the last few years of his life. Made a practice of cornering delegates with a fantastic plan of his."

Arnold drew back his papers, restored them to his brief case, and slowly zipped it closed. Supporting himself with the chair that he had been straddling so vigorously, he stood up to continue on to his own office.

"You came in here without even a 'good morning,'" Radovan chided. "Sit down again and we'll have some coffee brought up. I can see that you're the kind of person who's affected to an extreme by the environment. You strode in here all efficiency and nerves, carried the mood back with you from the UN." He clasped his hands on his desk. "Sit down," he repeated, "and hear some good news I've got for you," and waited until Arnold was seated again. "There's a bit of bad news, too, but it has nothing to do with you, just me, and it brought on the good news, so don't worry about it. Corby got through to Harringer to complain about you and what you wanted to say. Corby said that you had a nightmare oil painting in your head of humanity in the midst of orange flames and black ruins, and he said that if you had spoken you would have antagonized all the delegates as being holier than they, as being more hopped up about humanity, you know. Well, Harringer jumped down my neck. He was upset anyway, about the Hiroshima business, and he told me to bring you back from New York and then he said, 'What are we going to do with him now?' So I persuaded Harringer to send you out on your own, a grassroots sort of tour. As you know, Harringer's to tour the nation too, simultaneously, and he agreed that at his press conference before his tour he'll tell about yours. Like, 'My Secretary for Humanity, Arnold T. Elkins, is traveling the highways and byways of America, talking man to man with you, talking across the counter, on your doorstep, everywhere, to let you know, first hand, what we in Washington are doing for peace.'"

Radovan smiled a quiet, prolonged smile of accomplishment, the reflection of a smile that ought to have been on Arnold's face. "The tour will include Chicago, Kansas City, Denver, Seattle, San Francisco, Los Angeles . . ." sounding the names of the cities as one who has long dreamed of them but shall never enter them.

"But what of the conferences I'm expected to attend?" Arnold reminded him.

"There are always conferences," Radovan replied, "but this is more pressing. The Foreign Ministers' Conference in Geneva may fold up any day now, so there's no point in rushing you over there. If anything really important comes up while you're away, you'll be yanked right back home; you'll be the first delegate to arrive on the scene, wherever it is, London, Geneva . . ."

Arnold nodded his approval of the tour, possessed again by the concept of the post that had possessed him for the first time as he sat next to Flugeltaube in the reading room, the concept of it as more than that of its creators, an enlargement that justified whatever he would say or do on his own.

Radovan leaned back in his chair, shifting around in it self-consciously. "I'm sorry you and your family won't be here to attend my wedding. She's Amanda Eversledge, niece of our James. Her father is in construction—bridges, dams, shelters. The wedding is to be in Bucks County, that's where her family lives and my mother, too." He drew on his cigarette, his sucked-in cheeks emphasizing the hard little knobs of cheekbones. "We've known each other since we were kids, but off and on, you know. She spent her childhood in France and then went to Wellesley, and then when I was touring Europe, after Harvard, she was in the Near East, sketching. It was really only last summer when we both spent some time at home that we got to know each other." He smiled appealingly with his eyes, inviting Arnold to become a good friend. "Anyway, those are the boring details."

Arnold's congratulations led the young man to bring down from a cabinet shelf a crystal decanter of brandy. When they had drunk a toast to the marriage, Arnold, gazing at the brandy in his glass, spoke another wish to himself: Oh, may the Flugeltaube tribe to which I belong prosper, so that, among other results, Radovan and Amanda can bed down together and make merry together and bring forth flocks of children together who will dance on the flowering earth that the Flugeltaube tribe will keep under their feet with the triumph of its proposal. Overwhelmed at that moment by the memory of the opal-eyed old man of the United Nations corridors, he bowed his head in a sorrowing posture that passed, he knew, for the posture of one remembering the early delights of marriage.

5

The family boarded a long-distance bus at seven in the morning, with Radovan seeing them off and a photographer whom he had brought along taking pictures of their departure. The photographer posed Arnold with one foot on the step of the bus, his hat and brief case in hand, and in another shot, posed Arnold, Alma and the girls standing in a row against the side of the bus. The passengers, waiting in line with bundles and overnight bags at their feet, watched with puzzled curiosity. Arnold, as he posed, saw a sailor at the head of the line speak through the wire fence to the bus driver who was also watching. "How come *they* got in?" he asked. The driver informed the sailor, the sailor turned his head to inform the young woman behind him, and she, in turn, informed the woman behind her, who turned and informed whoever was next in line. At this point Radovan came out from behind the photographer and shook hands with the family in farewell.

Grasping Arnold's arm in fast friendship, he said in a low voice, urgently, "Promise me you won't let that expense account get you down. If you find you've got to expand a bit, don't worry. I don't suppose there's much range at those counters in the bus depots, but listen, don't hesitate to order yourself a steak when you feel like it, and that goes for the family. You're the kind of conscientious person who'd carry this deprivation business too far and imperil your health and morale. The key is moderation." His face was close to Arnold's and each small cheekbone seemed to be aching with concern.

After he had climbed aboard the bus with his family and while the other passengers were filing in and tossing belongings on the rack above, Arnold realized that the expression in his assistant's eyes had been an unfamiliar one, one never there before, perhaps. Was it a sense of loss? He glanced out the window to wave goodbye, but Radovan and the photographer had already disappeared in the crowd.

Through the blue-tinted bus windows they looked out upon the trenching machines at work along the highways, scooping out trenches for the concrete pipe, four feet in diameter, which, once it was covered with three feet of earth, was to serve as fallout shelters for those citizens who might choose to leave the cities in the quarter of an hour that was theirs to choose in after the warning and before the missile hit, or for those whom the warning caught on the highway in pursuit of business or pleasure. Arnold, his temple against the windowpane, tried to recall the figures he had found in the newspapers for the highway shelter system, but no exact figure came to his mind, dulled by the monotonous sight of cement pipes waiting to be laid within the trench. At night, he pressed down a knob on the arm of his chair, as his family and other passengers were doing, and was jerked backward into a reclining position. A young woman laden with white-cased pillows passed down the aisle, and he rented a pillow for each member of his family. In the dark morning, their clothes wrinkled, their teeth coated, and with sweat pockets under their eyes, they left the bus in Chicago, registered at a third-rate hotel not far from the depot, as their expense account dictated, and fell into their beds.

He awoke in midmorning with the day plotted out for him, his need to act having driven him to plan in sleep. He would call on the editors of the daily papers, and his importance as Secretary for Humanity would warrant an interview on page one, and in that interview he would say that, in his opinion, there was great need for all sides to consider compromises, big and little. He would appear to meditate, and then say aloud that he was of the opinion, also, that time was of the essence. If he said it slowly enough, after a pause long enough, they could not accuse him of being an alarmist. So excited was he with this calm and convincing self, that he took only a moment for a cup of coffee in a café next to the hotel and started off.

He found himself, on his first call, in the cold, puzzled presence of an editor who supported the other candidate for President, Emery Fixas. With an absence of spark, the editor lifted his eyes from the work on his desk, scanning his memory to place the visitor aright; then, bowing his head again to resume his work, began a long tirade against Harringer for the roadblocks he had set up in the path of the nation's defense. Every word that Arnold managed to get in edgewise reminded him of another roadblock, and soon Arnold rose to depart, thanking the editor for his sound advice.

The second editor, supporter of Harmon Harringer, greeted him with a modicum of enthusiasm, as he might have greeted a minor congressman. The editor, refreshing himself with coffee and glazed doughnuts, offered some to Arnold, and their eating together seemed to reaffirm the host's belief that Arnold was in accord with the administration, as was the editor. When Arnold spoke of the vast treasure consumed by weapons of war, the editor, nodding, suddenly emptying his cheek of a lump of doughnut, assured him that the nation's industry was, indeed, kept jumping with defense contracts, and that Harmon's insistence upon his defense budget and upon the shelter program had averted a major depression that threatened to follow upon the heels of the previous administration with its penny-wise, pound-foolish philosophy. The man construed as praise every word that Arnold spoke in criticism, listening receptively while wiping sugar flakes from the corners of his mouth, as if to someone reading back an editorial of his own, one that contained words of caution and advice to the Chief Executive within the context of encouragement. Arnold shook hands with the editor in fraternal farewell and descended in the swift, silent elevator, the sour aftertaste of sugared doughnuts rising up from his esophagus like the taste of old dreams that are better forgotten.

A nostalgia for campus grounds, a belief in the receptiveness of scholars to the call of reason, led him to the university, where he sought out the man who had been his philosophy professor fifteen years before at the University of Iowa. In the interval, Dunbar Dykes had become a famous figure, conducting a Great Thinkers course for executives—a summer course of three weeks' duration held in a lodge in the Teton Range of Wyoming, the students partaking of pure air, long hikes and philosophical discussion. His televised Sunday evening program, "Great Thinkers," in which he cleverly utilized props, films and guests to illustrate his lectures, drew an audience larger than that of any other program of that hour. Arnold, as he walked across the campus consulting the schedule of summer classes that he had picked up at the registrar's office, learned that the course conducted by Dykes as Lecturer in the Humanities was a short course designed to acquaint science students with other areas of human endeavor.

Arnold was rewarded for his half-hour of waiting in Dykes's office by a warm greeting from his former teacher, who grasped his hand and would not release it until Arnold was seated by his desk, close to the professor's swivel chair.

"I am honored! I am honored!" cried Dykes. "The Secretary for Humanity waits in my office to see me!" He had grown heavier in the intervening years, higher of brow, faded in color, yet more colorful, the way a famous person is emboldened by his fame in every wrinkle, every hair and crease of clothes, so that even a wen on Dykes's left cheek was a particularity of fame. "The student returns to bring news of the world to the old teacher asleep on his bench in the grove," he cried.

Arnold, taking as a cue this reference to the knowledge that he brought, began at once, commenting that man's progress in technology had far outstripped his progress in social relations. Spatially, he said, humanity was rising higher and digging deeper, but the rockets into space were launched to secure a military advantage and the blows into the depths of the earth were struck by man seeking to save himself from the enemy's missiles. As Arnold spoke, Dykes sat back, hands gripping the arms of his chair, eyes so shining with the impact of his visitor's words that Arnold had the uneasy feeling that his listener was overshooting the mark. "Unless," Arnold warned, "unless at this last moment man begins to draw up plans for living together, as diligently as plans are now drawn up for destroying one another . . ."

Dykes, nodding, interrupted him. "The tide is turning," the professor assured him. "Do not despair. To despair is to put yourself out of step with your own time. The sign that I find most encouraging, because it heeds that necessity to plan that you speak about, is the decision a few days ago at the United Nations to increase the budget of the Committee for the Control of World Population. Of all the UN committees, it is the most crucial, for if the human race continues its alarming rate of growth then the work of other committees, however diverse, comes to nought. You sound the alarm against nuclear weapons, but I hear a larger explosion than any thermonuclear weapon could ever produce—the population explosion. The CCWP sends mobile units into every backward country to disseminate literature on the disadvantages to the mother, to the father, the community, the nation, the world, of large families. The native doctors are requested to impress upon their patients the need of contraceptives and the Committee distributes the most modern and efficacious of these free of charge to the doctors who, in turn, pass them on to their patients. Billboards are set up in villages and cities to remind the citizens to equip themselves. The lack of doctors in these backward countries presented a problem that was partially solved with mobile fitting rooms for the women, each staffed by a nurse or two. All theories are being explored, such as the theory that a starch diet promotes fertility; so high-protein tablets are distributed, also free of charge, to those whose diets are restricted by poverty." His shining eyes were fixed on his visitor in a gaze that made Arnold feel derelict in his duty to mankind.

"It appears to me," Arnold said, "that we are in accord about the ultimate aim for humanity—no famines, no rabbit warrens—but that one of us is approaching it backward."

"Go on," the professor urged, unafraid of dispute. His compassion was the core of him, clear and hard as a diamond, and someone else's proof that he was at fault in his methods of ministering to his fellow human beings had the effect of buffing a facet of the inner jewel.

"You must realize," Arnold said, "that in this era a disarmament pact must be of a different sort from any in the past. A pact today must demand more than the dismantling and destroying of armaments. It must also demand improvements in the condition of man as a guarantee against the pact breaking down. A nation's prosperity would no longer be based upon preparations for war but upon preparations for—" he was about to say Utopia but changed his mind in favor of a conservative phrase, one that sounded less illusionary and more like something Dykes himself would say—"mankind's rich maturity. All signatories to the disarmament pact will be signatories to this enterprise and no field, no discipline, nothing will be neglected. One among the many projects will be population planning." He lifted his eyes to see the effect he was having on his listener and found that the bright gaze had dimmed.

"It sounds good, it sounds terrific," Dykes said. "But

when one asks who is at the steering wheel of this theoreti-
cal pact that boasts the solution for all of man's ills, whom
do you find? Karl Flugeltaube. My science major students
may never have read Shakespeare or heard of Tacitus, but
they know that Flugeltaube was one of the greatest minds
of this century and that in the last years of his life he lost
all powers. There's quite a spread about him in this week's
issue of *Explosion,* a pictorial analysis of his disintegration.
There's one particular picture of the old fellow in a corridor of the UN. The caption explains that the photographer had been snapping delegates and when the films
were developed, one came up with this bony figure in it.
His editor identified it as Flugeltaube. They kept it in the
files and used it in this obituary, and it's very, very revealing. Senile dementia, eyes gloggy as a fish's. There's another picture of his hotel room, cockroaches and crackers
in the drawers, cobwebs hanging from the ceiling, flies on
apple cores. That credo of his about never harming any
living creature can be carried to an extreme in a small
room. When he came out of the jungle to push this plan
of his at the UN, someone, one of the U.S. delegates,
pointed out to him the dangers to us in weakening our
defense and asked him if he was hankering to live under
Communism. His answer was of the kind that the very old
imagine is full of meaning, humorous and subtle, but
which only demonstrates their senility. He replied that he
would rather be alive than dead." Dykes shrugged. "It's
all in the article. Since I'm sure you haven't read it, I sug-
gest that you do. That was his answer, an answer entirely
forgetting mankind's long history of sacrifices for freedom's sake." He drew his chair close to his desk to slip some
folders into a drawer, decisively.

Arnold, after a few minutes of recalling with Dykes some
of the students in that class of years ago, stood up when

the professor stood up and walked with him to his next class. Beyond the closed door, the room was filled with murmurous voices.

"You, of all my early students, have come out on top," Dykes said, shaking hands in farewell. "However, let us return for a moment to our former relationship of teacher and student so that I can advise you to steer clear of the Flugeltaube group. I know that you are seeking a way out for humanity, and I commend you for it, but beware of answers that answer everything, as his does. Beware of prescriptions for the *elixir vitae*."

Arnold recalled that in his youth his heart had filled with Dykes's words of wisdom, for his words on any subject had seemed axiomatic, applicable to all subjects. Now there was no heart to swell in his chest. "Do you suppose," he ventured, impressing upon himself that he was, after all, the Secretary for Humanity and that he was not asking a favor but granting it, "that I might address your students as a guest speaker? This summer course in the Humanities is, I think, an appropriate one in which to bring up the subject of disarmament. I can simply touch on the history and ethics of the idea."

The professor smiled, closing his eyes as over some amusing malapropism of a lower classman. "That, my dear Arnold, would be cutting the ground out from under their feet. For six years they have undergone the most rigorous training in physics and its various branches, astrophysics, chemical physics, thermodynamics, and so forth. And, of course, before that, in high school, they were science majors. So one can say that their lives have been devoted to developing themselves into scientists so that they can make their capacity contribution to the defense of their country. I don't think they would give your pitch the consideration it deserved." Dykes gave Arnold's hand one last pump and entered into his classroom.

So distressed was he by his conversation with Dykes that he walked past his bus stop with his head bowed and took no notice of other stops until, at last, he paused to wait for the bus by the corner of a shelter excavation fence. Several men were gazing in at the apertures, and Arnold, gazing in also, saw an excavation of the entire city block. Way down at the bottom crawled dump trucks loaded with dirt, and three trucks, at that moment, rumbled down the street, carrying the dirt away. The man on Arnold's right held his stained felt hat in his hands to permit the noonday sun to bake his balding head. On Arnold's left was a thin and jumpy young man in a yellow and brown striped T shirt, his hair shaven on top and long at the sides, hanging halfway over his ears in the style favored by a rebellious juvenile element.

"Why we got to wait until the alarm blows before we can go down there?" the young man complained. "Them professors over at the college, they're worryin' about us, they say we got nothin' to do and no place to do it in. Well, hell, why can't we go down *there* when it's finished? I hear they're gonna have a gym to keep people's muscles from gettin' flabby and weak if they got to stay down a long time. What we could do is go down there and use that stuff, break it in. We could get familiar with the place. Then when the rush hour starts, we could act as ushers." Dreamily, he plucked at the T shirt over his stomach.

The elderly man on Arnold's right wiped the top of his head with a dirty handkerchief. "Summer or winter, which'll you guess?" he said.

"I beg your pardon?" Arnold asked.

"When do you guess they'll shoot 'em over here, summer or winter?"

Since the man seemed in earnest, Arnold mused upon it. "The answer involves, I imagine, a number of things," he said. "Such as strategy, the fortuitous factor . . ."

"I guess winter," the man interrupted. "They're bound to do it in winter because that's when you're sitting cozy in your own room and don't feel like going outside in the sleet and the wind. They know it won't be no fun running to a shelter. That's why I say we ought to do what the senator in the papers says we ought to do. We ought to wage preventive war. Prevent 'em. Otherwise, you give 'em a choice, they'll start everything in the winter time." He stuffed his handkerchief into a rear pocket of his trousers which once had been a navy blue and had faded to purple. "It'd be just like 'em to drop it in the winter. They're mean enough to do it."

Arnold, reaching for his cigarettes, sought the words that would convey his own sight of the excavation to these spectators. "Myself," he said, "I don't want to go down in the summer *or* the winter. Neither one, nor the spring nor the fall. The way I see it, all the countries ought to get together and destroy their missiles."

The young man's head seemed to be withdrawing, turtle-style, into his rising shoulders. His face was suddenly pale, defenseless, like the face of a person accused of a horrendous crime that he did not commit and has heard about only in the accusation. "It was *you* who said that, not me!" he cried, and ramming his hands into his pockets, walked away so quickly he appeared to rattle.

The elderly man fixed his dim blue eyes on Arnold's eyes, his thick old underchin shaking. "What did you tell that boy?" he demanded.

"That we ought to destroy the missiles," he began.

"You leave that boy alone!" The old man's voice struggled to free itself from the years' sediment of silence. "It's you sons of bitches that make those boys bad boys, telling 'em to destroy, destroy, destroy. You beat it now!" he cried. "If I catch you hanging around that boy any more, I'll call the cops!"

Arnold, noting in the man a tendency to panic, a desire to run and summon, rejoiced when in the next moment he heard the bus approaching. The realization came to him, as he faced the man, that Demosthenes had never placed real pebbles in his mouth in contriving to perfect his oratory. There was no need to, for the confusion in the minds of the listeners was like pebbles in the mouth of the speaker. He heard the bus brake to a stop and, turning, jumped aboard, compelled against his reason to feel and to act the culprit.

He threw himself face down on the bed in the hotel room, clasping his head in his arms to shut out the old man's voice. Since he did not hear his family enter, he was surprised by the rocking of the bed as Alma and Becky plumped down beside him. He turned over onto his back so that he would not appear to be suffering into his pillow, and Alma put three evening newspapers on him.

"There's nothing at all about you and your tour," she told him. "The President held his last press conference before his campaign trip and he spoke of lots of things, but you weren't one of them. No picture, nothing."

"I think I've been exiled," he said.

They were quiet for a moment. He saw Bernice, who was leaning her elbows on the high dresser and brushing her long hair in that preoccupied way of hers, bring the brush down slowly and turn her profile toward him apprehensively, and she seemed to be acting out his own awakening as he lay with his arms under his head.

"The triumvirate no longer loves me," he went on, smiling crookedly at the ceiling. "And they went to such pains in selecting the winner, too: for beauty, for wit, for absence of enemies."

"But you're in your own country," Becky said. "They always send exiles to strange countries."

"Ah, but they've done it this time, too," he replied, sitting up warily like a man with a sore back, making no move to rescue the newspapers slipping to the floor.

In the town of Canumbra, Missouri, between Chicago and Kansas City, the bus broke down. The passengers filed into the small waiting room with its wooden benches, magazine stand, and soft drinks machine, and sat down to wait for the bus to be repaired. Bernice, sitting wanly between her mother and father, complained to them that her ankles were swelling from her many hours of confinement on the bus; she ought to be lying down with her feet elevated, she told them. After Japan, she could no longer speak aloud her fear of the bomb, but the discomforts of the bus trip gave her an opportunity to speak complainingly of something more bearable than the bomb, and the family understood about the relief this gave her. And because he wanted her to know that he sympathized with her, and also because her desolate face was embarrassing to him now that some of the passengers sat facing them on the wooden benches, Arnold suggested that the family take a stroll in the fresh air.

They passed four blocks of business district to the west of the depot and, beyond an auto wrecking yard, found themselves by a concrete retaining wall overhung by tangled bushes. At intervals, recesses in the wall gave access to rickety wooden steps leading up to old houses and dry gardens. Alma pointed out that they might as well be knocking on a few doors in Canumbra, and Arnold, agreeing, gave himself courage by likening himself to a sentinel of the nation's early years, one who rode into town on his horse, shouting warning of flood or the approach of Indians. He thought: Canumbra is a small town and has no industry, but it won't escape, because it's on the periphery of both Chicago and Kansas City and will get the primary radiation when the missiles hit the big cities, and it may even get a missile itself in a saturation attack. At the next recess in the wall, he turned and led the way up a flight of gappy stairs stuck through with weeds, Alma and Becky coming after and Bernice remaining below.

Upon a high, slanting porch, he stepped over an upside-down red wagon to knock at the door. It was opened by a young woman to whose skirt clung three children, one, two, and three years of age. She was followed by a boy a few years older than the rest. One of the children at her skirt was using it to wipe his nose of the mucus running down into his mouth and, as she greeted the visitors, the woman pushed the child behind her. He reappeared among the folds of her skirt on the other side.

Arnold introduced himself and Alma and Becky. No light of recognition appeared in the young woman's eyes. "As your Secretary for Humanity," he said, "I'm knocking at your door to warn you of the danger that the town of Canumbra may find itself in, in the event of nuclear war."

She brushed a strand of hair from her eyes. "I'm not clear in my mind what you want," she said.

The oldest boy leaned against the door jamb. "If they kill us we'll kill them right back," he promised them all, his face one to be relied on. "If they get New York, we'll get Moscow, if they get Chicago, we'll get Warsaw, if they get Los Angeles, we'll get . . ."

The child with a runny nose gave a whooping laugh, baring his tiny teeth, then hid his face in his mother's skirt, swinging and laughing. The mother, grasping the older boy by the back of his shirt, struggled to pull him away from the doorway. She succeeded in thrusting him off to one side where the callers could no longer see him and, almost stumbling over the children in her skirt as she stepped backward, she began closing the door. "Could you come back some other time? Or you could leave me your card and I could vote for you. Is it more missiles you're wanting?" Afraid that she was treating them discourteously, she advised them with a kindly smile not to call at the neighboring house since the old woman living there alone never answered the door, fearing assault.

They descended the stairs, almost tripping on one another's heels. Bernice, rising from the bottom step, suggested that they return to the depot in case the bus had been repaired and was waiting, and they accepted this as an excuse to save themselves from further rebuffs, as she knew they would. They retraced their steps, no one speaking, and in the waiting room Bernice refused to lie down with her feet elevated on an overnight bag, for to be so conspicuous in her discomfort was like confessing the family's circumstances to the other passengers.

Arnold, seated again on a bench, drew from the rear pocket of his trousers the morning newspaper he had been reading when the passengers were forced to leave the bus, and read again, on the front page, that the Geneva conference was still in progress despite caustic disagreement among the ministers. He had been agitated enough while reading it for the first time in the bus's narrow seat, yearning to escape from his exile's journey and fly to Geneva, there to deliver that impassioned plea for concessions from all sides that he had risen, part way, to deliver at the Subcommittee session before the Swedish delegate took the floor away from him. Trapped in his bus seat, he had felt a resurgence of respect for that plea of his, as meager as it had seemed after his conversation with Flugeltaube. The first step, he had reminded himself, was to save the life of humanity by a ban upon the bomb; to try to save and improve it, both at once, by advocating the Flugeltaube proposal was not the first step but every step after that first step. Now as he reread his newspaper in the waiting room of the Canumbra bus depot, the bus's breaking down brought home to him his own condition. He was rising decisively toward the phone booth when Alma thrust at him, across Becky, the other half of the newspaper that she had slipped away from him a moment before, and he saw that she was pointing to the syndicated column of Clark Kapperby on the editorial page. He took the paper from her and was surprised to find that the column was devoted to him, or rather to an extract from an article in a Soviet periodical of humor and cartoons. The extract inquired into the whereabouts of the Secretary for Humanity, who had disappeared from the United Nations. He was not to be found in his Washington office, and no one in the Triangle knew where he might be located. Had he been done away with? the Russian humorist asked. Exiled to southern Utah, that highly radioactive area north of the Nevada bomb testing grounds, or shot? And why? Was it because he was already so obsolete before he was put on the market that nobody wanted to buy him? It had been rumored around the United Nations that Elkins was to appear on an ass, but this he had failed to do, and it was suspected that at the last minute he had balked at this Biblical means of conveyance, fearing that it would label him beyond doubt as an anachronism. No comment by Kapperby followed the extract, for no comment was necessary, it being common knowledge that Harmon Harringer, the man who had created this comic post, was not the columnist's favorite President, and that as soon as he was out of office, with Emery Fixas in his place, the columnist would be a happier man. Arnold folded up the paper and, gripping it like a weapon that had been thrust into his hand by some god or goddess on his side, entered the telephone booth by the soft drinks machine and sent a collect call to the number in Bucks County, Pennsylvania, that Radovan had given him.

A woman servant answering the phone informed him that Radovan, his mother, and his sister were all at Amanda's house, the Newton Eversledge residence. He requested the operator to put him through to the second number, collect, and after some delay, during which the telephone at the other end passed through the hands of a woman servant, a small boy, two elderly women, and a man who identified himself as Agnew and who told the operator he was expecting a call from New York, at last the voice of Radovan was carried to his ear, a faraway voice, a young voice, courteously pleased, inquiring after the health of the Elkins family and expressing anxiety as to the family's whereabouts.

Arnold plunged into his complaint. "Radovan, there's no point in my wandering around the country like this. Nobody listens to me, nobody knows me. A man can't work by himself any more. That was all right in the Bible days when the prophets came into the cities with their beards and their goatskins. But not now. And even if they listen, what can they do with it? I spell out the handwriting on the wall and nobody knows what to do with it. Listen," he pleaded, cracking his knee against the wall as he shifted his long legs in the metal booth. "You remind Eversledge that I'm supposed to be an extra delegate to every conference. He promised me that wherever men of two or more nations sat down together to discuss disarmament, I'd be the third party or the eighty-sixth party . . ."

"What're you writing on walls about?" Radovan cut in, unbelieving. "Nobody suggested that to you. All you're supposed to be doing is knocking on doors . . ."

"Listen! Did you see Kapperby's column today?" He lowered his voice. "The Russians are making the most of my disappearance. They say I've been shot because nobody wanted to buy me." (That, he thought, ought to hit the boy where it hurt most.) He paused, and receiving no reply, went on, "The Geneva conference is still going on. I could make my reappearance there."

At last Radovan replied, his voice vacuously alert, as one hearing confused alarms. "The morning paper got away from me," he said. "We've been busy all morning with photographers, Amanda and I. Tell you what to do," he said. "Eversledge isn't the man to see on this"—attempting a note of innocuous conspiracy against their chief. "But Harringer isn't available. He's campaigning in Illinois and then he's going west—Texas, California, Washington, Oregon. Tell you what to do. When you get into Seattle, give me another call and by then I ought to have some news for you. You won't make the Geneva conference, of course, but there'll be others. Is there anything else troubling you?" he asked, and the question, translated by the oversolicitous tone of his voice, meant that he had already heard enough and was anxious to be alone with it.

Arnold hung up and, a-steam with nervous perspiration, left the booth. He saw that the passengers, including his family, were picking up their wraps and filing out to the bus platform, and he followed them out, the last in line, yearning to believe that his assistant would get through to Harringer and persuade him of the wisdom in Arnold's call. If he were given a chance to speak he did not doubt that he could convince all nuclear nations to unload their bombs into the Mindanao Deep. He saw himself at the rail of the lead ship in the U.S. procession, and saw the other processions, all flying their flags, converging with his. And in that hour, he said to himself as if remembering, trees were planted by the children of Japan, by the children of France, by the children of Nigeria, by the children of Canumbra. . . . His conjuring head bowed, he climbed again aboard the bus.

When the bus broke down again not many miles beyond Canumbra, the passengers were assured that another bus was leaving Hannibal, Missouri, that very moment to pick them up and carry them, express, to Kansas City. In the matter of an hour they would be on their way again. The other bus did not make the scene, however, until almost midnight, when the cheerful voice of the driver roused the passengers from their shallow, twisted sleep. Arnold, wakening to the green light of a highway sign pulsing through the bus and to the sight of dangly-limbed children carried out over the shoulders of their elders, was terrified by the thought that the bus had fallen beneath the waters of the Mississippi; and the fact that the smiling driver, standing up front, had everything under control, persuading the passengers to behave in water as ably as they did in air, only increased his terror. Becky, standing up beside him, pushed her knee into his legs, for he was barring her way to the aisle and the exodus, and he came completely awake in time to swallow his nightmare cry.

6

In a torpor from the ride, Arnold gazed out upon the edge
of Kansas City, Missouri, as the bus entered the city in the
dark hours of early morning. The familiar billboards that
he had glimpsed in every city were repeated here. Among
the ads for local hotels and restaurants and automobile
agencies, for beers and oils and cereals, was the NIX-R ad,
the anti-radiation pill, with the large calm face of a beautiful girl gazing skyward toward a missile arcing over the
horizon and with the familiar words: CUTS DOWN HARMFUL
EFFECTS BY AS MUCH AS HALF IN SOME CASES; the Blue

Champ Dog Food ad with its forlorn cocker spaniel against a background of human beings striding toward a shelter sign; and an ad for Daisy Powdered Milk, the product of a state whose milk contained less strontium 90 than the milk of any other state. As the bus sped onto an overpass, Arnold underwent the sensation of entering at full speed into a billboard that shone spectacularly before them, larger than the others. From out of a black, whirling chaos, huge red letters trumpeted:

RICKY ROUNDUP
PALACE AUDITORIUM NOW

Arnold's cramped chest filled with frustration. The evangelist Roundup had no difficulty finding an audience. His agents preceded him to give releases to the press, to hire the largest halls, to set up his name on the most conspicuous billboards. But Arnold T. Elkins was preceded only by whoever got off the bus ahead of him.

Again, because of weariness and limited funds, they chose a small hotel not far from the depot. As unraveled and wrinkled as the family appeared, they had a look of gentility about them that prodded the desk clerk. A fat fellow, his arms shortened by his bulk, he had difficulty slipping on his sports jacket as fast as he wished to.

Arnold shaved that morning in the communal bathroom across the hall from their rooms on the second floor, leaving the door open to permit some air to enter the cubicle that reeked of disinfectant derived from pine trees. A woman guest had kissed the mirror, leaving the print of her mouth in lipstick, and he did not remove it, titillated by the sight of his face with the red kiss on it, the only act of love and gratitude bestowed upon him on his journey.

After he had made his unavailing rounds of the editors,

he called on the program chairman of the Excelsus Club, a club whose membership, merchants and men of industry, was one of the largest in the city. Here he requested time to speak at the club's next meeting which, a news item had informed him, was to be held at noon of the following day in the Venetian Room of the Hotel Marple. But the program chairman, a manufacturer of shoes, whose office walls were shelves of sample shoes from toddlers' up to the black oxfords worn by elderly women, informed him that the speaker for the next day's meeting was the New York architect of Kansas City's exciting new Giant $ Store which was to be erected next year. The manufacturer, a man of brusque gestures and affable smile, each of these qualities canceling out the effect of the other, said that the plans called for a store half above ground and half below ground, three floors above and three below, the floors below to accommodate the home furnishings department, tearoom, child care facilities, gym equipment, rest rooms, and so forth, so that they might serve as a comfortable shelter for those persons shopping within the store or near the store at the moment of the alarm. Of course, the walls were to be of adequate thickness in concrete. The décor, he said, was to be Hawaiian—lots of bamboo and plants and colorful murals, and he had also heard that ultraviolet lights were to be installed throughout to promote suntans for the clerks. Wherever a new store was contemplated to replace one that had become too small for an expanding community, the Giant $ Store Corporation was to utilize the plans of this imaginative young architect. The question period for a guest like that, he said, usually ran the meeting up to five o'clock. Rising and shaking hands again with Arnold, he wished him good luck on his tour, assuring him that he would find leaders of industry, merchants big and small, all on their toes for the nation's defense.

"You heard Roundup yet?" he asked.

"Not yet," Arnold replied.

"We had dinner with him last night at the Mayor's, the Excelsus officers and wives, and we were all impressed. That man Roundup—biggest mind in America, got a real grasp of the totality. You know? *God has given us time to prepare*—when he says that, you get an idea of the tremendous role of this nation and your own role in the whole thing. You don't have to be a rockets expert to do your bit. You know what I mean? When it comes time for the Alliance Shoe Manufacturing Company to build a new home, we'll consider building it underground. The main task before us is to keep our corporate identities in the event of war. If we do, if we come up again with our corporate identity intact, we'll be doing our part in retaining the nation's identity."

Arnold, transfixed in that moment of parting by the benignly close yet insular face, was thinking back to his day in Hiroshima, to the great mound of the dead, to the dead who were beyond recognition even if there had been relatives to recognize. Would there be mounds, he wondered, in every city of this nation? The nation's identity and all the corporate identities might be retained, but what of the mounds of the unidentifiable dead? He thought of these mounds as the last barrows of the age of inhumanity, the biggest mounds and the last. In the outer office, above the clacking sounds of a typewriter and the metallic grating of file-cabinet drawers and the distant rattle of machinery, he took his leave of the program chairman, promising to relay to the President the Kansas City Excelsus Club's aggressive participation in the defense of the nation.

At Bernice's insistence, the family that evening sought out the Palace Auditorium. They were swept up by the crowds pouring into the huge amphitheater in which rodeos and ice follies were held, popular singers made personal appearances, and candidates for political office spoke at rallies. After climbing several flights of stairs, they came out up near the rim of the oval-shaped theater and saw that every seat below was occupied and that around them, in the upper area, seats were filling up fast. Young people in white clothes with blue armbands acted as ushers. It seemed to Arnold that the place was filling up as if at a signal, and thinking of trumpets, he heard a trumpet blown. At the south end of the arena the trumpeter appeared, a long, blue banner with white letters hanging from his highly polished instrument. Marching across the sawdust to the large platform in the center of the arena, he was followed by a never-ending line of choristers in white garments who, once they were assembled on the platform, began, to the strains of a hidden organ, the Roundup hymn that had become a popular song: "Take God Underground with You." The organ and the many voices were so thunderous that the family had difficulty in making out the words except for the phrase, *When you go down, down, down into the shelters, You rise up, up, up to the Lord*, which was repeated in the chorus and had already made its mark upon their consciousness via the jukeboxes in the lunch counters of the bus depots. As the last strains of the organ faded away up near the ceiling and the chorus seated itself on the several rows of chairs, a boy carried upon the stage a small, worn, walnut lectern from the church of Roundup's boyhood in Robling, Idaho. He set it down in the center of the stage and continued on across, and for several moments all was hushed in the vast theater as audience and chorus awaited the appearance of Ricky Roundup.

In a black suit, a white Bible in his hand, he strode across the sawdust and mounted the stage, laid his Bible on the

lectern and a hand on each side of it. He was an excep-
tionally tall man of about six feet four, and his curly black
hair added two more inches. His face was large and pointed
of chin, and the set of his head, along with the pale stare
remembered from his portraits, gave him the aspect of a
high-soaring bird, an eagle, a hawk, that sees a panoramic
view below. Since he was, however, such a tiny figure in
the vast theater, the Elkins family, up near the rim, could
not see his features, could not see his mouth move, and
his voice, emerging from the loudspeaker near the ceiling,
took them by surprise, as a voice from the sky.

After he had greeted his audience and the entire city, and
had offered thanks to the Lord for urging his audience to
come, he began his sermon with a sudden swooping-down
voice. "Never before," he said, "have so many people,
numbering in the millions, been on the move in one direction at one time. The greatest migration in the history
of mankind is to be the migration underground into the
shelters. This descent," he said, "will be the most profit-
able migration in history. When the whistles blow, when
the thunder rises from millions of feet running for the
shelters, when the cries of small children and the infirm
fill the air, we will have no fear, if we know that, though
we perish, though many of us perish, those who survive
shall climb again to the surface with a renewed love of the
Lord in their hearts. For the Lord has stayed the enemy's
hand long enough to give us time to prepare our weapons,
to dig our shelters, and He will be there to accompany us
down. And as we assemble in our shelters, we shall see
proven to us as it is written in Romans 8:38—*For . . .
neither death, nor life, nor angels, nor principalities, nor
powers, nor things present, nor things to come, nor height,
nor depth, nor any other creature, shall be able to separate
us from the love of God. . . .*" He threw back his head,

and his small gaze from way down in the arena seemed to fix itself upon the Elkins family. "Man's descent into the bowels of the earth shall be known as the great descent that was the ascent. Let this Nuclear Era then be known as the Age of Ascent."

The evangelist was quick of tongue, abhorring pauses of great portent, like one who has much to say that is pithy and usable at once. He went on to tell of the plaint he had heard again and again from pastors throughout the country. They were troubled, he said, by their inability to stem the tide of violence within the country: the increase of big and little crime, of juvenile delinquency, of traffic fatalities, of murder, of suicide. Among some psychologists, he said, the "catastrophe theory" was gaining ground, the theory that the prospect of mass extermination induces in the potential victim the desire to create a personal violence of his own choosing in order to assert his individuality. Roundup's advice to those pastors who came to him for help was this: They must acquaint their flocks with the positive or ascending view of the descent into the shelters. Those on the verge of violence must be made to anticipate with joy the mass descent.

When Roundup concluded, the ushers passed the collection baskets and, into one, Bernice dropped all the coins from her purse; she had no paper money. The chorus rose and sang again, a hymn composed by Roundup, "We Are Not Here but Are Risen," and children in the audience began waving the blue programs. The adults joined in, until all over the theater blue flags were waving, resembling the surface of the sea agitated by opposing winds and currents. And the organ and the chorus of three hundred voices were like the sound of the sea, the rhythm that is present beneath the surface chaos.

Upon their return to the hotel, as Arnold and his wife

were saying goodnight to the girls in their room, Bernice, under the covers, reached out to Alma, pulled her down to sit on the bed and, giving a short wail, laid her head in Alma's lap. "But I can't help it!" she cried, explaining her need for dropping coins into the basket. "It makes me feel that we'll be all right. I mean, if I say that I think Roundup has a point and donate something, when we get down into the shelter we'll get to come up again. You know what I mean," she wailed angrily at Arnold in the doorway. "You can explain it right back to me better than I can."

Chastened by her anger, he said nothing. But walking up the hallway he recalled the letters he had read that first morning in his Triangle office, the involute letters, and it seemed to him that those who gave their pennies to see the light in the time of the deepest darkness were also some-how of the same direction, their edges curling inward. He climbed into bed, thinking of Flugeltaube and the scientists who had together worked out in infinite detail their proposal for conversion, and he knew that Flugeltaube, who had desired that men unfold and save themselves, would, had he come to Kansas City, have been confined to a place for small and peculiar gatherings, with no music to accompany his vision.

No sooner had Alma got into bed beside him than down in the narrow alley a brawl began. The thump of a garbage can struck by a falling body was the first sound, followed by curses and groans—unbearable sounds, like a wardful of invalids fighting among themselves. Arnold leaped out of bed and wildly flinging aside the curtains with their suffocating smell of decaying cloth, stuck his head out the window and shouted down the word *Stop*. But the frustrations of his journey warped his voice and made the word a riddle. He tried again to shout the word, but discouraged, drew back and crawled into bed.

The next morning, as the family waited at the corner to cross over to the bus depot, sirens sounded through the noise of traffic and the way was cleared by six motorcycles for a large, new convertible of buttercup yellow in which sat Ricky Roundup and his wife. When the car had passed on its way to the airport and the sirens had faded into the distance, the family crossed over, given a green light.

As the bus approached Denver, Colorado, early in the afternoon of a clear day when the distant mountains were detailed as after rain, the bus driver, shifting in his seat, turning his head a bit, yet keeping his eyes fastened on the highway, spoke to the passengers. "Today's the day they go under," he announced.

The passenger immediately behind him, a small, graying man in a dark suit, replied in a high voice that conversed with the other passengers as well as with the driver, "That ought to be a holiday, locked up in a big shelter like that with free food, lots of room to move around in. It's those prisoners from Folsom Penitentiary that volunteered to stay down in that little quonset hut under the ground, one hundred of them in 24 by 48 feet—now *that* was something! The decent way they behaved showed the rest of us we could stay down in something like that, too, when the time comes. This thing here in Denver is just to show off Denver."

"Denver's my city, too, mister," the bus driver said loudly, his shoulders swelling in his tight, whipcord jacket, and the rest of the passengers laughed, as if he had made a clever move in a game of wits against the man behind him.

"It's when people is cramped together that it means something," the passenger persisted, his voice cracking under the strain of a camaraderie he did not feel.

The driver nudged upward the visor of his whipcord cap. "Denver's beat every other city and you know why? Because we got a head start. Nobody has to be ashamed of a head start, not in this business, because it means you saw farther ahead than the rest of the country. Six, seven years ago some guys in Denver got the idea of using them abandoned hard rock mines up in the mountains for storing records, and they dug them deeper, 150 feet down, 200 feet down—good blast protection. Now there's federal agency records down there, city records, corporation records—anybody can rent space there. They even got executive quarters down there, little offices, little apartments, for Denver executives to hole up in. The old miners who walked out of there last wouldn't recognize the place." He swung the bus around a car pulling away from the curb. "Well, after work begun down there in the mines, the whole city decided it was going to dig in, even before any federal aid came through, and began the big downtown shelter on its own. And that's why we're through before anybody else. As it says in the signs you'll be seeing, Denver leads the nation."

They were, indeed, greeted by sign after sign, flaring above the intersections, and passing under these windy banners, Arnold folded up his newspaper and penciled the location of the shelter into which the twenty-four winners of the letter-writing contest, conducted by the newspaper on his knee, were to descend. They had given the best reasons for: *Why I want to participate in the shelter program.* A motion picture for nation-wide televising was to be made of the assembling in the shelter, and among those notables who had consented to appear and to wish the winners well were the Vice President of the U.S., the Governor of Colorado, as well as the Governors of California, Texas and Nebraska, the state's U.S. senators and several of its

congressmen, and a famous movie comedian. Lars Skiverveer, chairman of the Civil Defense Committee of the
Defense Department, was making every effort to be present
to congratulate the city of Denver for its wholehearted
contribution to the defense of the nation.

In the hope that he and his family would gain admit-
tance to the ceremony on the strength of his Triangle
pass and that he, as Secretary for Humanity, would be
able to say a few words on the screen—even if his appearance were to be deleted, still he would have made an
attempt to impress upon the audience an alternative to
the groundhog existence they faced—he hustled his family
off the bus before the other passengers, hustled them into
a hotel, where they deposited their luggage, and then
hustled them into a taxi, afraid that they might already be
too late to make their dissenting appearance below.

After a mile ride into the heart of the city, they arrived
at the shelter entrance just as several notables were emerging from beneath the banner. Among them Arnold recognized a congressman who had been a guest at the dinner
held in his honor that first night in Washington, D.C., and
he put out his hand. The congressman and his family, a
blond, pleasant-faced wife and a boy and girl of high-
school age, all recognized the Elkins family with a show of
pleasure. The congressman explained that the television
film was over and that most of the guests had already departed, but in the few minutes before locking-up time the
family was welcome to go down and look around. There
was coffee and cake down there, he said, and cocktails for
the adults. He was an energetic, affable man and he did a
sort of sideways skipping step to the policeman at the entrance, instructing him to permit Arnold and his family
to enter the shelter.

The family descended the long stairs which had several

turnings, and were very wide to accommodate a rush of people, their footsteps echoing against the walls since they were, for the moment, the only persons using the stairs. The room which they entered was enormous, its concrete floor with lines of white paint, similar to a gymnasium floor. High on the wall facing the stairs was a large window through which could be seen a bare-headed young man in an army shirt and a young woman holding a baby over her shoulder and patting its back. The young man was drinking coffee while perched on the edge of something, a table, perhaps; they could not be seen below waist level. The observation booth, Arnold guessed, from which instructions would come by loudspeaker to the crowds entering the shelter. Lowering his eyes, he saw many doors with signs above them reading: TO RESTROOMS, TO FIRST AID, TO RECREATION, TO LIBRARY. . . . A small party was in progress against the left wall, or it appeared small in the vastness of the room. Long tables were laden with party foods on white cloths, and from two shiny coffee urns the fragrance of fresh coffee was wafted to their nostrils.

At the same moment that Arnold and his family saw Marybeth Crockett in the group by the tables she saw them and came forward at once to greet them, no less delighted with their appearance than she would have been with that of the James Eversledge family. As she approached, Arnold was made conscious of their rumpled clothes and unpolished shoes. They were, he saw, altogether lackluster, and for a moment he was embarrassed. It seemed that in opposing her they had roused the anger of the gods whose emissary she had been, and now they wandered in exile, barefoot and bedraggled victims of their own willful natures. But none, he saw, were penitent. Bernice had lowered her head but hers was a gesture of disassociation; she hoped to convey to Miss Crockett that she was innocent of what the others were guilty of.

"Ah, but you're late!" cried Miss Crockett. "You should have got here a bit earlier for the movie. We've had lots of celebrities but we never expected to see the Secretary for Humanity and his family. Would you like to meet the people who are going to stay down until next Sunday?" she asked, taking Bernice by the arm. "They'd love to meet all of *you*."

"Is Denver your city too?" Alma asked, falling in behind her and Bernice.

"It is for this week!" laughed Miss Crockett. "I'm acting as hostess down here, or chaperon, or whatever you want to call me. They've got a young Army captain and his wife to supervise—and they've got their baby with them, too!—but Skiverveer thought I ought to be here, too. It was his idea. He said, 'Get over there with some advance copies of the White Cloud book to give out to the celebrities,' so we rushed some off the press and rushed me over here, and there I was, handing out copies to the Vice President and to the Governors and all the rest. The television movie will serve as its debut to the public, you see? It's exciting, isn't it?" she asked Bernice, squeezing her arm. "You should have met George Fringle, he was so funny. You know that fast way he talks? One minute he said this was the biggest stage he'd ever appeared on and the next minute he said if he had to stay down here he'd get claustrophobia! You really can't repeat what he says because it's the *way* he says it, isn't it?"

Bernice, heedless now of her parents' disapproval, asked, "Who did you get for the picture?"

Miss Crockett gave a little cry of delight. "Can you imagine? We got the Eversledge family, James and his wife Marcella, Sally, who's eighteen, and the two sons, James, Jr., and Ogden, eleven and thirteen. The children's faces are so bright, and oh what a beauty Midge Eversledge is! That clean-cut kind of beauty, you know. The Skiver-veer family was the choice after yours, but he's got just one son, a junior in high school, and the son looks just like his father. Besides that, his wife and he resemble each other, too. So it didn't work out for that family. But after the Eversledge family consented, we all agreed it was the best choice after all. The wife and children of men like Eversledge have to learn to be in the limelight, too. We're *all* participants in the nation's defense."

They had come into the midst of the group now and, raising her voice, she introduced the family. The contest winners said their how-do's from wherever they happened to be. Two teen-agers, a girl in white pedal pushers and red sweater and a boy in cords and an orange jacket with "Denver '66" on the back of it were bent over a game of Scrabble, sitting on their rolled-out sleeping bags on the floor; and a very old woman, gray curls misting a pink, balding scalp, was knitting on a bench, her back against the wall, yarns unrolling among the coffee cups and tri-angle sandwiches. She smiled at them so youthfully, so artlessly, that they were rendered speechless. What an honor it is for her to win over so many thousands of younger persons, Arnold thought; it is the crowning achievement of her life and has restored her youth. The other winners, whose ages were between the two extremes, were standing around the tables, popping into their mouths the many kinds of delicacies. One of them, a red-haired fellow whom Miss Crockett introduced as a dentist, appeared with a tray at Becky's elbow.

"Punch and cookies for the girls," he announced, "and Explosions for those over twenty-one! It's a Collins with champagne substituted for the soda," he explained wink-ingly to Arnold. "You've only got a minute before all visitors clear out, so you'd better not hesitate. He who hesitates is lost," he warned, prodding Alma gently with a corner of the tray.

Alma's gloved hands refused to unclasp themselves from around her purse, which she was pressing against her bosom as if it contained an external courage. Since all the other notables had departed, most of the contest winners were gathering in a circle around the Elkins family, and Alma, fixing her gaze upon one particular young woman because she could not cope with the entire group, said to her, "What's all the celebrating about?"

The circle of celebrators fell silent, gazing at Alma with the fixed look of those who have not heard aright. But Miss Crockett, her arm around Bernice's delighted shoulders, was happy to explain, for to her the question was not at all irrelevant, coming as it did from someone who appeared always to be emerging from the hinterlands. "These people are celebrating their participation in the defense of Denver and the nation," she explained. "They won the contest because their letters stressed their desire to help their fellow men by demonstrating what a human being can endure under hardships. They are proud to serve as models."

Alma's hair needed a washing; she had forgotten to visit a beauty shop back in Kansas City. One dull lock fell from under her small, nondescript hat. Her face was in need of rest. The journey was taking its toll. Arnold put his hand upon her arm to convey to her the fact that he was more persuasive than she, that his mastery of the art of lecturing entitled him to the precious time, but Alma, unwilling to relinquish the moment after she had grasped it by the forelock, pried away his hand with her fingers. "Some contests," she began, raising a fear-cracked voice, "are better avoided than won . . ."

Quickly he lifted his chin a bit to signify that he was to speak, and he *did* speak, addressing them in smooth, friendly, urgent tones; but at that moment a piercing whistle was blown, a blasting high note that set his ear membranes to flapping like the banners in the streets. His audience turned their eyes upward to the high window where the young captain could be seen, hand on hip and police whistle to his lips, and their excited laughter and exclamations resounded against the concrete walls.

"Time to go, visitors," the officer said, his magnified voice separate from him and with no source; and closer, like an oboe against a background of deep orchestral sounds, Miss Crockett's voice was crying, "It's locking-up time! It's time to leave us all alone!" And with a sweet, maternal extending of her arms, she rounded up the lingering guests.

The contest winners now crowded around the departing Elkins family, Alma's few words rendered meaningless by the group's desire to part from the visitors in a state of high-pitched friendliness. They trotted along beside the family, stepping on their heels, and the dentist with his tray urged them to drink down their refreshment. The young woman to whom Alma had addressed herself, a young woman in a gay flowered dress cut low over her breasts and a pink sweater on her arms to keep out the coolness of the depths, was jogging along beside Arnold while kissing her husband who was departing with the Elkins family.

"He came down with me, they said he could," she explained to Arnold breathlessly. "They said he could stay for the party because we've just been married a couple of weeks." And she turned suddenly toward her husband's insistent face, forced by the tightening of his arm around her and by his hand's covering of the breast that was closest to Arnold and that had been bobbing against his sleeve. "I'm glad that camera went away!" she managed to cry, and those around the couple shouted their laughter.

The group remained at the foot of the stairs, for the ascent was long. Only the wife went up with her husband, borne upward in the steely grip of his right arm, and it was not until the voices of the persons below were fading out and the couple tarried behind them at a turn of the stairs that the absence of Bernice impressed itself upon the rest of the family. They listened for her footsteps and, hearing nothing, Arnold ran down again, passing the couple in silent struggle in an angle of the stairs, hidden from those below and those above, the wife striving to remove her husband's hand from between her thighs, her face delightfully rosy over her husband's shoulder.

The trouble with himself, Arnold thought, as he ran on down, was that he had always taken everything too seriously—ideas and people, everything. He had never learned to toy with anything. Everyone else—the Scrabble players, the couple on the stairs behind him, the dentist with the tray—enjoyed themselves, and if, as he suspected, Bernice was staying down deliberately, he could sympathize with her: she remained to enjoy the chatty, comforting atmosphere wherein people toyed with the idea of catastrophe, fancying themselves, by the nature of the toying, in control of that catastrophe.

The persons below had gathered again around the tables, and some were picking up paper plates and crumpled napkins, the cups and glasses of the party. Nowhere among them was Bernice, nowhere her red jacket and long pale hair. Cupping his hands, he shouted, "My daughter's down here!" and his voice echoed back and forth against the concrete walls.

Miss Crockett ran in her high heels toward the door marked RESTROOMS, but emerged a minute later shaking her head. Arnold turned to shout back up the stairs, cupping his hands again: "Go on up the rest of the way and tell them to wait!" his voice hitting Becky full blast on her way down to assist in the search. Then he ran for the door marked ART AND CRAFT SUPPLIES, the door to the left of it entered by Miss Crockett and the door to the right by Becky.

The room he found himself in was a storeroom with thousands of games stacked on shelves. Three women were chatting around a counter, perched on stools and leaning on their elbows, their voices enlivened by the confidential closed-off room. "The strangest thing was that the girl next door won a contest last year, six hundred and fifty dollars in the state finals of a cherry pie contest," one woman was saying, "and when I won this contest, nobody could believe it. Next door like that. It's proof that good things don't happen just to your neighbor, to somebody else. They can happen to two people next door to each other." After a glance around, under the counter and down two narrow aisles that the shelves made, he withdrew and, emerging, heard Becky calling to him. He traced her voice to the First Aid room and, entering there, found his elder daughter huddled on a hospital bed, clinging to a sheet-like curtain that hung down from rings on a rod, a curtain that had served to conceal the bed. She was weeping into it, hiding her face in a futile attempt to conceal herself again.

Arnold put a firm hand on her bowed shoulder and she sat up, smudging the bed linen with her dirty heels. Again on her feet, she began to wail dismally. Becky untied a silk scarf from her neck and pressed it into her sister's hands and the offering was accepted gratefully, he saw, for it had been presented with gentle urgency, a token of apology from Becky for the years of her needling and poking.

And with the scarf muffling Bernice's wails, they went out across the white-marked floor to the stairs. A gigantic, amused voice that was portentous of the nation's reaction when the newspapers were to tell of her escapade rolled them along like a wave: "A stowaway, a stowaway, a stowaway, eh?"

When they reached the top of the stairs they found the young bride standing with her back to them, her face thrust through the opening of the shelter door which was big as a boxcar door. Hearing their footsteps behind her, she partook of one last kiss with her husband whose face they could see through the opening. Through the narrow space, they also saw the crowd behind him and the several cameras, there to record the closing of the door, moving in as close as possible to that last kiss, and heard the crowd beyond cheering this display of matrimonial affection. The young woman drew back, her face even rosier than it had been on the stairs, and Becky stepped out first, followed by Bernice, head down, the wailing subsided and the tell-tale scarf stuffed into her pocket, and Arnold came last. Alma reached for her elder daughter's hand and, together again, the family pressed and pushed its way through the crowd and, exchanging no words, rode a bus back to the hotel.

The newspapers that evening gave over their front pages to the shelter experiment, and vying for first place with the notables and their congratulations to the city was Bernice Elkins, daughter of the Secretary for Humanity, who had tried to stow herself away in the First Aid room. The details of her escapade were telephoned up from below, and by AP and UP the story reached all corners of the nation. She wept a good part of the night, desirous of changing her milieu yet unhappy that her attempt to do so had worked against her parents' intentions for their journey. Becky came into their room in the early morning to report on her sister's condition, and they found themselves as observant of *her* condition as she was of her sister's. They saw that she was feeling pity for Bernice, the first human being to arouse it spontaneously; up to now, she had felt it most deeply for small animals. And they saw that she was brooding and she had never brooded before, more inclined to hassle with an opponent than to hassle with herself. And, watching her as she sat at the foot of their bed, telling of her sister, Arnold began to wonder if she brooded because she had no tangible opponent, nobody to thump on the head, verbally, for driving her sister to hide in the shelter and to weep half the night for doing it. Whoever she might choose to thump was nowhere around.

They left Denver that morning. To seek for an ear to listen to his plea was, to Arnold, as futile a task as speaking against the piercing whistle in the shelter. The city was keyed-up, incontrovertible, for deep in its bowels were its noblest citizens and strung from every telephone pole and lamp were the banners of its distinction, Denver Leads the Nation.

They boarded a bus for Helena, Montana, a family pledged, all except Bernice, to a major accomplishment, a pledge that encouraged them to perfect their minor accomplishments in the art of bus travel—where to put the feet, how to lay the head to avoid cricks, which side of the bus to choose in order to avoid the heat of the sun.

On the outskirts of Cody, Wyoming, the bus was flagged down on the highway to permit a file of trucks to enter the gates of Air Force property where an intercontinental missile base was under construction, one of the many all over the continent. From the window Arnold saw nine persons walking back and forth at the open gates and, his breath quickening, he read the signs that a few of them carried. CONSTRUCTION WORKERS! DEATH IS YOUR PAY-MASTER! read one sign. WAR IS THE ENEMY, said another. The lead truck idled at the gate while several Air Force guards dragged aside the obstructors. Along by the high, barbed-wire fence, twenty or more men and women were ranged, drinking soft drinks from bottles. One of the women pulled her tight skirt up her thighs to give her legs more freedom and tripped a young man in jeans and skimpy jacket, carrying a sign reading NO MORE WAR. When he fell, the molesters shouted so loudly that the noise buffeted the window against which Arnold's face was pressed. A man standing next to the woman sprang forward to assist the young man to his feet, but once he was up again the Samaritan kneed him in the buttocks, sending him flying into the picket ahead of him. Arnold rose from his seat but sat down again as he saw another woman, a matronly woman, her large breasts bustling within her red print cotton dress under an open coat, approach and embrace the youth. For a moment Arnold believed that she was comforting him, draping one arm around his shoulders and sharing with him the contents of her bottle, but as he watched, the woman poured the liquid down inside the boy's shirt and immediately his shirt and the fly of his trousers were wet and dark. In this condition he continued his walking when the woman released him, still holding his sign aloft.

Arnold rose again, pushing Alma, who was sitting beside him, along in front of him. Calling for his daughters to follow, he swung down the bus steps. Tossing their few pieces of luggage against the fence, he fell into step with the pickets who were forming their line again before the closed gates. Alma, followed by Becky, fell in behind him, but Bernice sat down on the luggage to watch from afar with owl's eyes. A few feet ahead of Arnold walked the boy in jeans and, tapping him on the shoulder, Arnold offered to carry the sign and the boy passed it back to him. The bus and the cars behind it went off down the highway.

The rough handle in his hands alarmed him. What a scandal, he thought, if it were discovered that Arnold T. Elkins, Secretary for Humanity in the President's cabinet, had jumped off the bus to join these obstructors! It was one thing to plead for disarmament and another to set himself up as an obstacle before a U.S. missile base. And who were his companions, on second thought? They might be agents of the enemy. From the corner of his eye he saw two men in dusty jeans and cowboy boots, one bare-headed and the other in a Stetson, leave the line of hecklers and approach him, and in the few seconds left to him he decided that he would not resist, for if he struck his attackers and injured them he would be arrested and his identity discovered. And he was glad that these persons he had joined seemed disinclined to resist their tormenters, for he was compelled by more than courtesy to act as they. So he permitted one man to hold him from behind with encircling arms and the other to rip off his tie, unbutton his collar, and pour the contents of a soft-drink bottle down inside his shirt. Before the bottle was empty, the large woman in the red dress stepped forward with another bottle, and before the second was empty she called for a third. It was brought by a young woman who elbowed her aside when she reached for it and, gripping his belt, drew it out from his body far enough to admit the neck of the bottle. The cold liquid ran down his stomach, down his legs, and into his shoes, and his wet clothes adhered to his skin. Alma and Becky, he saw, were bristling to come to his aid but were held back by his own nonresistant behavior. The other hecklers called cheerfully to him, urging him to persevere. The fact that he was in a dark suit and hat, in contrast with the other pickets in casual clothes, aroused in them the desire to lay him low, to deny him the respect they thought he felt was due him because of his clothes. They wished to impress him, this genteel fellow jumping impetuously from the bus, with the hardness of life's knocks. Someone removed his hat and poured several bottles of a lemon drink over his head; he smelled it as it ran down his face. They released him, then, and he began his pacing again, holding his sign aloft, his teeth clamped so tightly together that a few minutes later, when he relaxed a bit, he discovered his jaw in rigor.

The young man slowed his step to permit Arnold to catch up with him, and Becky came up from behind to join them in a line of three. "They're from Cody," the young man explained as they walked together. "The town is prospering. The soldiers, the construction workers, all spend their money there and the town shows its appreciation in this way. For Cody's sake, I'm sorry we're so few. It's like somebody saving your life and you pay him back by making a big to-do about brooming the mouse under his chair."

"How long do you keep at this?" Arnold asked.

"We do it for half an hour more," the boy said. "We have an exact quitting time, so nobody can think we've been routed."

"I admire your persistence," Arnold said, drawing a handkerchief from his wet trousers to wipe his wet eyebrows. "Who *are* you?"

"We're pacifists," the boy replied, and told him that they were encamped in tents not far away, where one of their group washed and dried the clothes and kept a pot of soup cooking. They had picketed the base for three days and would continue for another two, and then they would pack up and proceed to Gallup, New Mexico, where ground was to be broken for another missile base.

"It does seem impractical to me," said Arnold, "that you would attempt to prevent a war by walking in front of a truck."

"It's to the point, isn't it?" the boy asked, his slender, parrying presence recalling for Arnold the students he had walked with on the campus at DeVelbiss.

"Oh, it's to the point all right," Arnold replied, pressing his coat sleeve to halt a dripping, "but is it effective?"

"Some day a laborer may walk off the job," the boy said.

"One laborer?"

"Some day," the boy went on, "we hope that our numbers will be so great—" he paused in his pacing for an undetectable moment to shudder in his wet and sugary condition—"so great that this nation will disarm itself."

Arnold took it from there, eagerly. "The United Nations," he began, "must enforce a . . ."

But the boy interrupted. "I'm talking about this nation alone." The soft drinks had, here and there, made mud of the ground. His light tennis shoe caught in a patch of it and he paused to jerk his foot free.

"Alone?" asked Arnold.

"Everything we've got, down to the lead bullet." His foot slipped out from the shoe and he wriggled his foot back into the shoe and, again, tried to jerk it free. This time it left the clutching mud.

Arnold could not rouse himself to move. These persons, whom he had joined to help them defy their tormentors, seemed to him bereft of their reason, and for a moment he felt inclined, not without shame, to examine the point of view of those who were abusing them. "Ah, but the recklessness of it!" he exclaimed. "I believe in disarmament, but through negotiation. We disarm while the others are also disarming." He was forced to walk again by the coolness of the late afternoon air.

"This country would give as its reason the immorality of war," the boy explained.

"The immorality? Just that?" Arnold asked, almost stumbling over Becky who was walking sideways and a bit in front of him in order to hear the young man.

"That's enough, isn't it?" the boy asked.

"But," Arnold persisted, "isn't it immoral for us to leave ourselves undefended?"

The boy pointed to a pickup truck coming down the highway toward them. "The man driving that truck is a pastor," he said. "He'll refer you to Romans 12:20. '. . . if thine enemy hunger, feed him; if he thirst, give him drink; for in so doing thou shalt heap coals of fire on his head.' What that means, he says, is that if a country disarms itself, then the nations that are still armed will feel the evil of their arms like coals of fire on their heads."

The truck braked alongside the pacifists who climbed aboard, crowding together. The boy invited Arnold and his family to spend the night with them, assuring him that there were canvas cots and blankets for everybody and promising that Arnold's clothes would be dried for him during the night. Since he was reluctant to enter the town of Cody in wet clothes and, by registering at a hotel there, reveal his identity and his participation in the pacifists' activity, Arnold accepted the invitation, and he and his family climbed in among the others. All of them, those who were wet and those who were sitting against the wet ones, shivered in the wind as the small open truck rattled up the road to the encampment. Arnold, packed in between the youth and Alma, his legs bent up to make precious room, saw them all as misfits. They were, he thought, as absurdly few as the early Christians had been in their time, and with that thought he realized that those who had conceived of his role would not be pleased with his fulfilling of it in this way, jogging along with odd companions, with wet and draggled company, in the back of a pickup truck.

They were recognized by several of the pacifists as the Arnold T. Elkins family, and after he had related to them his history in the office of Secretary for Humanity, they were more than eager to see to his and his family's every comfort. The family sat on army cots and were plied with steaming hot lentil soup in tin cups and bowls, and with bread that was somewhat stale and hard but tasty. The members of the group were of all ages, from the young student whose sign Arnold had borrowed on up to the elderly man who tended camp, small and spry and eighty-three. And the ten of them, men and women, had come from as many points of the compass, by bus, by air, by hitchhiking, by car, to meet together and picket for one month several of the missile bases under construction along the Rocky Mountains. The student told Arnold that he was from the nation's capital and that he had bought a car for fifty dollars from a used car lot and that it had performed without a hitch all the way across the country. Arnold saw that three other cars, in addition to the pickup truck, were parked on the edge of the camp, and something about one of them reminded him of the car that had been given him that morning of his arrival in Washington, but the twilight was deceiving, wrapping the car in the dust-gray memory of another.

When they were lying upon their canvas cots piled over with khaki-colored blankets smelling of garages, of oil and of musty forgotten things laid away, Alma called his name in a whisper. "There is something in my nature," she said when he had grunted his wakefulness, "that makes me hit back."

"It must be a great discipline," he said. "I am sure they have the same inclination to hit back at those who attack them. One gets used to it." A flea had hopped from the blankets into his sweater, and at the same time that his shoulder twitched he chuckled. "It's not less than spectacular, isn't it? To see them refuse to return violence for violence."

"No, it didn't appeal to me, hanging around behind you when the deluge came," she went on, "and it wouldn't do for me to join any group like this because some day I'd disgrace them all by tearing away with tooth and nail." In her agitation she moved under the blankets, stirring up their dust and odor, and was forced to cover her nose.

"It's a time of extremes," he mused, gazing at the stars through the branches above him. "After years of improving the weapons of war to destroy more people in less time, we have reached a kind of ultimate weapon, or the first of that category, with the missile and the bomb it carries. Such extreme violence needs something else extreme to come to grips with it." He scratched the flea bite on his shoulder reflectively.

"Guess I got it from my father," Alma said apologetically, shifting the blame to somebody else. "You know Casey. Worst-tempered man in Langshank County." She tried to settle down comfortably.

After a while she was quiet, no more fidgeting, and he fell asleep with the cold stars breathing on his cheek, trying to keep him awake like a host of revelations.

7

They arrived in Seattle in the middle of September, at noonday. As they rode up in the hotel's jittery elevator cage, Arnold read the headline of the newspaper that the operator had tucked into the railing next to him: *Harringer to Dedicate School Shelter*, and read in the column beneath that the ceremony was to take place at two o'clock that afternoon at the Grace McMahon Elementary School. Suppose, he thought, as the operator tugged open the elevator doors at the fourth floor, suppose he were to attempt to speak to the President? And he hurried his family down the musty hallway elatedly, as if they had proved their mettle down hotel hallways across the country and this was to be the last.

The family, alighting from the bus before the small, red-brick auditorium of the school, were at once claimed for the ceremony by the loud, smacking noise of the U.S. flag whipping in the drizzly wind at the top of its pole and by the muffled music of a band playing within the building. As they climbed the steps to the arched doorway, a troop of little girls, pink party dresses peeking out through unbuttoned gaps in their raincoats, swarmed past them, their voices shrill and gaspy. Inside, the students occupied all but the last few rows of seats and these were taken by parents. Along both sides stood teachers and more parents. In the area below the footlights, a high-school band in vivid green uniforms was playing the national anthem. At the left of the open stage a television camera roved its eye over the audience, and at the right three chairs waited.

The Elkins family joined the row of parents and teachers standing at the back and, as the last notes of the anthem knocked brassily against the ceiling, the President appeared on the stage, flanked on his right by an old man with thick bangs of gray hair and on his left by a young man with a balding head. For three minutes the audience, standing, applauded the beaming trio and gave in slowly and grudgingly when the youngest of the three at last signaled to them to be seated. Introducing himself as the principal, Albert Olson, he said that the school was honored that day by the presence of two great men: Harmon Harringer, President of the United States, and Ordon Watts, the school's most famous alumnus, proud possessor of the title Father of the ICBM, and a graduate, fifty-four years ago, of the Grace McMahon Elementary School. They had come to participate in the dedication of the first school shelter in the city to be completed, a ceremony televised to the nation. After the speeches here, he said, the President and Watts would lead a group of twelve students, the two highest in scholarship from each class of the school, down into the shelter where cameras were waiting. At the shelter entrance, the President would unveil a statue of Ordon Watts, commissioned by the School Board and executed by the sculptor Nicolaides Hart of Vashon Island in Puget Sound. The shelter, he said, was located under the playground, its entrance just behind the gym, and when the program in the auditorium was over, all would reassemble upon the playground. "And don't forget your umbrellas!" he cautioned them, and everyone laughed, the children finding a pleasant, nervous equality in the principal's desire to please their parents and to impress the President, beside him. After the laughter had dwindled down to a few scattered hoots from boys wishing to prolong it, the principal turned toward Harringer. After the ceremony, he said, the President was scheduled to board his private plane to return to the nation's capital, ending his visit to the city of Seattle, which was highlighted by his speech last night at the civic auditorium. His appearance at this ceremony, the principal said, transcended politics.

Arnold's desire to speak to the President, to unburden himself of the experiences he had undergone since his appointment, to trace the genesis of his convictions, and to evoke again, for himself, that feeling of great potential that the letter had stirred in him, this composite desire grew stronger with each moment of watching him shifting stolidly on small, nimble feet, smiling, nodding his round gray head at the clapping audience.

The silence that was given the President when he spoke his first words was even more respectful than the applause.

No child stirred, no adult coughed, and the fluttering of
lights up in the domed plaster ceiling was like a teacher's
anxious whisper to be quiet when no admonition was necessary. He said that he was happy to be present at this
city's first school shelter dedication. The hope of any nation, he said, was always symbolized by the children of
that nation. The protection of a nation's children assured
the future of that nation, and of all futures the most precious was that of the democratic nation. "Among you
now," he said, "are those who will be leaders of tomorrow,
and those leaders and their wise electors will find protection in the shelter that the present leaders and electors
have built for you. You," he said to them, "are posterity,
and in the shelter the thought to keep with you always is
this: Like a seed taking root in the earth in time of ad-
versity, you shall grow stanchly and truly, and in time
flower as only the children of freedom can flower." He
stepped back, beaming his appreciation of the applause
and sat down in the chair again. The principal arose, and
when the applause had ceased, introduced the scientist,
who at that moment was confiding a few words to the
President, tilting his head toward Harringer who was tilting
his head receptively toward the scientist while still smiling
his thanks at the audience.

The missiles expert paced back and forth as before a
blackboard, a small, slender fellow with a young, jaunty
way of tossing his hair from his eyes. With a dry, lively
voice that bespoke a mild nature, he said that he was honored by Mr. Olson's designation of him as the school's most
famous alumnus, but he would recount for them not his
own career but that of the giant missiles, a career that, in
a modest way, he had helped to further. It was necessary,
he said, to give them a history of bombing so that they
could see just where the missiles belonged. That history

began with the early TNT bombs dropped from airplanes upon the cities of Guernica, Rotterdam, Nanking, sorties that in spite of some protest from persons unwilling to accept a new dimension to warfare, proved their worth as a means to victory. With aerial warfare, he said, great damage that would prove astounding to the generals of history's classic battles could now be inflicted upon the enemy. For example, the incendiary raid on Tokyo by United States planes on March 9, 1945, destroyed 83,000 persons in one night. The next giant step was the atom bomb which, in its demonstration over Hiroshima, Japan, destroyed and injured an estimate of 200,000 persons. And the next step after that, he said, was the H-bomb, the thermonuclear bomb, representing what scientists call a quantum jump. But even as the H-bomb had within it the atomic bomb to act as detonator, the H-bomb was itself improved upon with a uranium shell and became the Superbomb, the first of which was exploded at Bikini in 1954. The latter bombs, he said, were popularly called H-bombs also. Just one of them could destroy an entire big city like London, for example, smash it flat within a circle twenty miles in diameter.

He was now out upon the apron of the stage and, as if startled by his audacious location, he folded his hands modestly behind him. "We now come to the subject of rocketry," he said, "because right along with the development of the bomb, scientists were working on the missile system of delivery." He glanced at his wristwatch as if afraid that the topic so captivating to him might prove boring to his audience, and said that he would list only a few of the advantages of the missiles. They were, he said, almost instantaneously ready and they reached their targets in a matter of minutes. Furthermore, the past few years had seen exciting developments in the solving of the re-entry problem and the speed of impact was now so great that the avoidance of radar detection and antimissile attack was a possibility within the grasp of our scientists. In conclusion, he assured his audience that in no aspect of missile development was the U.S. lagging behind the Soviet Union and that in some the U.S. had got there first. "You can say," he said, "that we're ahead of them by a nose cone."

While everyone was applauding, three little girls in pink frocks began to dance anxiously out from behind the curtain to the right of the stage, believing that they had been introduced and that the applause was to welcome them. Aware that the rest of the troupe was not following, they ran back. The principal, in the midst of kindly laughter from parents in the audience and derisive laughter from the boys, announced an entertainment by the girls in the first and second grades of the school, and the entire troupe danced out, the three premature ones losing their identity among the many. They were the little girls that had run up the stairs around the Elkins family, and to a potpourri of music from a piano down in front of the stage and hidden by the high-school band, they danced in and out of intricate formations, each holding a long limber stick to which a balloon was tied, the intermingling and separating of balloons an attempt to demonstrate in dance the fission-fusion-fission process, an effort that was explained afterward by the principal for those in the audience who had not perceived it. Urging them to be orderly, he then announced that everyone would reassemble on the playground.

The reassembling was chaotic, with children, parents, teachers, band members, all striving to extricate themselves from the mass and form again their own groups. The rain was now a fine needling mist and only a few umbrellas were up, most of them over teachers and grandparents. Arnold, taller than most, searched over the heads of the others for the President and saw him approaching the shelter, flanked as before by Watts and the principal. At the shelter entrance, which resembled an oblong concrete tomb like an Egyptian mastaba, the President threw off the opaque plastic covering from the statue to reveal a carven cedar-and-mosaic image of Watts holding in his arms, like an infant with a pointed head, a stainless-steel replica of a missile. The honor students were assembling behind the three men, entangling their small selves with Secret Service men and television personnel. Arnold serpentined his way through the crowd to the front row. A stretch of asphalt lay between the crowd and the shelter entrance, and in this area the band was entering into a green, flashy formation to entertain the crowd while the tour was conducted below. Arnold seized the present moment as the most opportune. If he went across now, he figured, he might loom onto the television screens all over the nation. The words that he would say to Harringer were ready on his tongue: *May I speak with you a moment? I am your Secretary for Humanity, if you recall . . .*

He was striking out into the clear space around the band when a little girl in a pink frock and red raincoat, one of the dancers, ran in front of him, darting out from the band's shifting mazes. They fell together, he hard upon his elbow, a result of striving as he fell not to fall upon her. He was assisted to his feet by a boy student in a yellow slicker and by three members of the band, and at the same time several teachers ran to pick up the girl who was crying in high wails, her nose skinned and the front of her dress crumpled and wet. Once again upright, he saw that the President and his party had descended, the last of the honor students disappearing, and he permitted the boy to lead him by the sleeve to the lavatory. There the young guide left him, running back to the ceremony. The basins were so low that he found he had to bend himself into a right angle and to bend his knees also, which were trembling with the shock. He filled his cupped hands with cold water and splashed it over his face, and after wiping his face with a rough, brown paper towel, he made his way back to the crowd, found his family, and left the school grounds, with the brass music of the band growing distantly discordant upon the misty air.

They returned to their hotel where Alma, enervated by a cold she had caught the night of the Cody encampment, crawled into bed. Bernice made bouillon for her, dissolving the cube in hot water that had been heated over a tiny, portable electric unit they carried with them inside a suitcase, after which she lay down on the other bed to read a paperback novel she had bought in the depot at Helena, Montana. Arnold and Becky chose to take a walk.

The operator of the elevator, an old fellow shriveled by the heat of the lobby's oil stove before which he read newspapers between elevator trips, greeted them as he opened the wrought-iron door of the cage. "What's your Geiger count today?" he asked them, and chuckled, deaf to any answer because the question was satisfying enough.

"You worried about it?" Arnold asked hopefully. A small item in the morning paper he had glanced over up in their room had reported a substantial increase in radioactivity in the rainfall, due, the item said, to the great number of bomb tests conducted throughout the summer by all the nuclear nations.

"We're the Fox in a Fix," said the old man happily as the cage shimmied down. "We stuck our heads into it like the fox in the water jar. We're all in a fix together and there's nobody going to get out of this no matter if he's clever or rich or got pull. Mr. Fox in a Fix, that's us."

Out on the sidewalk Arnold saw that his daughter was walking with her head down and her hands in her coat pockets, and he realized that he, too, was of the same posture and that it was not merely a response to the wind from the sea.

He cleared his throat. "It seems everybody likes the idea that the final fix will include everybody," he said. The passengers next to him on the buses, the waitresses behind the lunch counters, the hotel clerks, so many of them had the same comment, each seeming to find some kind of sustenance in the fact that he was not alone. "Let me ask you, why does a person take this grim, corner-of-the-mind comfort in the knowledge that if he gets the bomb everybody else gets it, too?"

"I don't want to think about it," she said.

"Let me think about it for you, then," he offered. "Is it because each person believes, some more and some less, that all his life he's been in a fix of his own and that almost everybody else is doing better? Ah, how sad!" he muttered. He took off his hat, for it seemed to be impeding his thoughts, and bent his head into the wind. "Ah, how sad that each one is wrapped up in his own troubles as in a cocoon and no one in touch, no one in touch with the rest of humanity."

"What do you want me to do with that?" she asked him. "It makes me feel worse, as if somebody told me my mother wasn't my real mother but was an inmate of an insane asylum who'd run away and kidnaped me and raised me crazy. That's the way those pacifists made me feel, like I was raised wrong." She hunched up her shoulder, stared down at her trudging feet. "I need galoshes," she told him, "if we're going to be wandering around all winter."

They walked on, Arnold mulling over her comment on

winter and wandering. "I could phone Radovan now," he said. "He told me to phone him when we got to Seattle. I think he may have persuaded Harringer to resurrect me since it's bad for the boy's career to let me fizzle out. It's not to Harringer's advantage, either."

They entered a café and found an open telephone on the wall. As he waited with the receiver to his ear for the operator to put him through to Bucks County, he took notice of his daughter's appearance as she stood near him, having refused the chair he had motioned her to. He saw that her face was thinner and that the fringe of black curls along the edge of her brown beret had grown untidily longer. The voice of Radovan's mother leaped into his ear, joyously informing him that her son and his wife were honeymooning in the Caribbean and that they had told no one the name of their retreat. She kept him on the line for a long while, cordially assuming that he was an old friend of the family who had been prevented by his diplomatic duties from attending the wedding, plying him with details of the event, who had been among the guests and what had been said and, gaspingly, just as he was hanging up, she called him ₊ack to tell him to purchase a copy of the current *Explosion*. Four pages, she said, were devoted to the wedding. *Raddy and Dandy Get Married* it was titled, and the photographers, she told him, had taken a picture of Dandy sitting on a big tree limb in a summer dress, dreaming of her wedding to come, and another picture of Raddy, in a white shirt and light trousers, strolling by himself along a stream and also dreaming. They had taken an especially lovely picture of after-the-ceremony, with the bride in her yards and yards of white veil like a lovely sea nymph in the foam, Raddy on one side and her Uncle James on the other, the three of them walking arm-in-arm under the trees. The last picture, she said, was of the couple boarding the plane to the Bahamas, waving, and Arnold knew without seeing the photograph, for he had seen others of couples waving, that the readers of the magazine fancied that they, too, were members of the family to which this charming couple belonged and that they, too, were being waved at. At last Mrs. Wells bade him goodbye, wearying of her affection for him, and he hung the receiver on its hook, overcome by the frustration that crawls in the flesh of the exile when he hears news of home. He opened the door for his daughter and they passed from the bacon-frying, shrimp-frying smells of the café into the street.

"I guess he didn't talk with Harringer?" she asked.

"He was busy with his marriage," he told her.

"Maybe he tried to, but Harringer was busy with his campaign."

"That may be." They went on a few steps. "But if you want to know," he said, "I think Radovan disowned me and fled to the Bahamas."

She stopped to stare down at her shoes again, as if they were refusing to permit her to continue along at her father's side. "I guess I'll go back now," she declared, and the abrupt way she turned told him that she was tired of his company, of his theorizing that only made her feel worse, and of the ease with which other people disposed of him.

Arnold glimpsed her through the sidewalk throngs, a small, stocky figure in a tweed coat wrinkled across the seat from a continent of miles on a bus. When she was lost to his sight he turned away and continued to walk against the cold wind off the sea, reluctant to return, fearing that his presence was not a bolstering one in the dreary hotel room. He spent the rest of the day wandering the docks of the ship canal, for the thousands of fishing boats, heavy-timbered, seagoing ones and small, makeshift ones, and their thousands of masts intrigued him with their implication of a wider world and led him to remember the morning when the pages of names and thumbprints (strangers' names and strangers' thumbprints, all assuming that he recognized them) had showered down around him.

All the next morning, in a phone booth off the hotel lobby, on a wooden seat like a ledge, and with twenty dollars in coins in several piles at his fingertips, he tried to locate a Presidential secretary who would convey to the President his desire to report. It had come to him in the night, lying awake, that the departure of his aide was not a loss and did not leave him stranded; he felt, instead, that an obstacle had been removed. As a cabinet member he must certainly have instant access to the President if the message he brought was urgent, and when the time was granted he would convey that which he had asked his aide to convey. The cheering decision of the night was expressed for him in the morning by the ringing and clinking of coins falling into the box. Impressing upon each person with whom he spoke the urgency of his call, he was passed up through several layers of secretaries, and at last was heard by a man of clear and gentle voice who recognized him as a personal friend, someone who had stopped to chat on his way to the Presidential suite. It was unfortunate, said the assistant, that Arnold had not managed to make contact with the President in Seattle, as Harmon had just returned from that city. After quoting Harmon's summary of his campaign tour and his prophecy of re-election, as if this were the subject uppermost in the mind of the caller, he inquired the name of Elkins' hotel and the number there and asked him to remain within hailing distance for the next hour. All that hour Arnold sat in the booth, the door flung wide for air. The ring so long awaited (awaited, he felt, for all the days of his government career) brought an instant tremor to the hand lifting the phone from the hook. Far down the line a girl's voice, a clerkish voice reading a memo, left a message for Mr. Arthur Atkins. The proper party for him to contact was a Mr. Elkins T. Radovan, Secretary for Humanity, with offices in the Triangle.

They remained in Seattle for three more days to allow Alma to get the upper hand of a fever, and in that time he did as he had done in the other cities across the nation. Then he escorted his family aboard a bus for San Francisco, setting himself and them the task of continuing the tour. One never knew, he told himself, how many seeds took root behind one. They got as far as Kirkmire County in northern Oregon and there Alma took a turn for the worse and they were forced to quit the bus at the town of Wapson.

Opening the umbrella over his wife to protect her from the rain, Arnold led his family up the main street to the hotel, a capacious green frame house of three stories with a veranda and a landscaped front yard that was like an apron too small. In the lobby, once a parlor, an oil stove was burning within a marble fireplace whose figuring, a black grain within the white, resembled mildew. After Alma had been put to bed and given antihistamine pills, and the girls had settled down, reading magazines on the other double bed in the large, rugless room, Arnold put on his overcoat again and went out into the rain. He had noticed that the office of the Wapson *Times* was situated a few doors from the bus depot.

A thin man in a homey coat-sweater was leaning over the plump shoulder of his secretary at her desk when Arnold opened the door, setting a little bell to jangling somewhere above his head. Arnold introduced himself, expecting to be invited into the inner office, but the editor remained where he was, straightening up but not extending his hand, his head held stiffly sideways, suspiciously, in the way that some persons react to salesmen.

"Washington sent me out here," Arnold began.

"You got identification?" the editor asked. "Some guy came in here last spring, told me he was Vice President Rafferty, Smilin' Ed Rafferty, out grassrooting. Looked just like him too. Young, that kind of face like a hawk smiling, quick way of speaking. So I interviewed him, and the Portland *Chronicle* picked up the interview. So did the Seattle *Herald*. He said a lot of things he never said to anybody else. Said them to me. And then the real Rafferty blows his top." He held out his hand for the civilian pass to the Triangle which Arnold had taken from his wallet. "This means zero," the editor said, glancing at it, flipping it over. "Anything can be forged." He fixed an inquisitorial eye on Arnold. "You want to tell me what you're selling, right off? I'm a busy man and we can save time if you don't just stand there, shining your light in my eyes."

Arnold felt his neck reddening. "What I'm selling," he said, reining in his anger with a drawl, "is this idea for saving humanity . . ."

"Shelter blueprints for rural areas?"

"Yes," said Arnold. "Blueprints for the best kind of shelter."

The editor lifted his head high to stretch the tendons of his neck. A kind of exultation had taken him over. "You got a discrepancy in your story," he said. "First you introduce yourself as a cabinet member from Washington, D.C. Then you say you're selling blueprints."

Arnold gazed at the man, feeling his shoulders slowly slumping, feeling his resistance to the delusions of others dwindling down. The stare of the editor stripped away from him all higher intent, all humane partiality, and left him a stranger to himself and to the town, damp of overcoat, crafty of face, the aim of his existence being only the coveted things that a petty crook fixes his heart upon.

"You staying at the hotel?" the editor asked. "Then get on back there, because somebody's going to be waiting for you." He tucked the Triangle pass into his shirt pocket under the sweater. "This I'll keep as evidence," he said. "You'd have it torn up by the time the deputies arrest you for impersonating a federal official and trying to sell government blueprints we can get free any time. All a person needs to do is write to the U.S. Printing Office. Ask for blueprints for rural bomb shelters."

The door did not close securely, and to prevent the rain from blowing into the warm office Arnold stood out on the sidewalk, fussing with the knob, while the bell jangled inside, until the door remained shut when he removed his hand from it. As he walked back toward the hotel, he thought about the pass that the editor had confiscated. He could, he thought, go to the police and ask that they claim it for him, but they would ask him why the pass had been taken from him and entangle him further in the coils of the editor's fantasy. Perhaps, he thought, he ought to let the pass go. What did its loss matter? It admitted him to the Triangle but what was he doing there anyway? As he turned up the path to the hotel, he felt a sense of relief at the loss of the card. He felt that he would never again set foot on the black-and-white tiled floor of the Triangle lobby.

While he paused in the shelter of the veranda to remove his hat and shake the rain from the brim, a dark-green car with an insignia on the door came to a screeching stop at the curb and two deputy sheriffs rose out and up in a kind of graceful timing. They came up the path, their shoulders touching, and one commended him for removing his hat to them and the other put his hand under Arnold's elbow to guide him to their car. Arnold asked if he might inform his family, but this request only amused them. They could not imagine why a man whose business required of him such great mobility should burden himself on his excursions with a wife and children. They were both tall young men of equal girth and both had rosy faces, and as he was hustled down the path between them he felt that they were arresting him in order to bring him health, to feed him their nourishing diet and instruct him in their invigorating exercise, and that this regimen was the open sesame to a more livable life.

They deposited him in a cell in the basement of the redbrick county courthouse, where no sun entered and fluorescent lights burned by day. He sat down on the cot, the morbid feeling of acceptance that had come over him in the Wapson *Times* office preparing him now to endure twenty-four hours of confinement and a dumping-out at the edge of town, treatment which he imagined was Wapson's way of punishing a migratory crook. Leaning back, he remembered that he once had a dream of himself as the great arbitrator. It had been in those weeks when he was preparing to move his family to Washington, and in that dream his most formidable opponent, the party most difficult to persuade, was the Soviet Union. But this was no metaphorical box he was sitting in, erected around him by that country's delegates. This was a cell in a county jail in the state of Oregon. He lay down, tucked his arms under his head and, giving in to an exhaustion both physical and spiritual, closed his eyes against the ceiling that assailed him and slept.

Becky appeared half an hour later, her face beyond the bars of his cell the first sight that met his eyes as he awakened. A merchant across from the hotel had witnessed the arrest on the veranda, she told him, and had crossed over to tell the hotel clerk about it. Arnold related his experience in the Wapson *Times* office, refused an attorney, and pleaded for a cup of coffee and the daily newspapers to break the cell's monotony. She was longer on her errand than he had expected her to be and when, at last, she reappeared in the corridor she was without the coffee. She held a folded newspaper in both hands and, with a sleepwalker's look of having been dispatched by a dream, she approached his cell.

When he reached between the bars for the newspaper, she bowed her head, refusing to give it to him, and he saw her tears dropping on the gray linoleum floor. "I didn't mean to make trouble for you," she said.

"In all your life you've never made any trouble for me," he assured her. "It's been a pleasure."

"But now I have," she said.

"All I asked of you," he told her, "was that you ask the deputy at the desk if your father could have a cup of coffee. What kind of harm can come of that?"

"Not from that."

"Then from what?"

She wiped her eyes with one hand and handed him the newspaper with the other hand, a gesture contrite and dull, like that of someone resigned to an incapacity to remember more than one thing at a time. "From the letter I wrote to the New York *Times*," she told him. "That day in Seattle when I left you on the street and went back to the hotel, I wrote it then. This Portland paper has some headlines about it." She gazed down at her hands that she had cupped at the level of her waist. "It surprises me that they made so much of it."

Unfolding the newspaper and, with it, blotting out her unhappy figure, he saw the high black headlines:

and read in the release that the accusation had been ringingly made by the presidential candidate at a giant election rally in Madison Square Garden the night before.

"Arnold Tennyson Elkins may yet prove to be the most infamous traitor this country has ever warmed at its unsuspecting breast," Fixas warned in his televised address. "One can read easily between the lines of this childish letter appearing in the Letters to the Editor column of the New York Times. *One can see the heavy, traitorous hand of Elkins upon the hand of his little daughter, Becky. In this letter Elkins instructs the American people to hold up their empty hands and be victimized by armed robbers, he pleads with them to surrender up their freedoms to the invader.*

Arnold lowered the paper to look again at his daughter. She was still gazing down, fiddling with the buttons on her tweed coat, her beret pulled penitently low over her brow.

"What did you say in the letter?" he asked her.

"You can read it, it's there in a box," she told him.

It was, he saw, enclosed within a thick black border in the center of the front page. He read:

Dear Editor:

What is wisdom? It is knowing a lot. We like to think that our country knows a lot. But also I think wisdom means that you can doubt that you are wise. The time has come for us to doubt that we are wise, because we are now in trouble. I am speaking of the bombs.

If we do not admit that we are not wise then we are idiots. Also, if the Soviet Union won't, they are idiots. This also applies to England, France, West Germany, China,

Turkey, Spain and all the other nations who have the bomb. *The first nation to destroy its bombs will prove that it is the wisest of them all. I would like to see my own country be wisest.*

I have given this subject a great deal of thought since my father became Secretary for Humanity.

Yours very truly,
Becky Elkins

Arnold drew a long shaky sigh of apprehension. "You got a discrepancy in you," he said in gritty imitation of the Wapson editor. "You say wisdom is *it* but you haven't learned anything since the day we got to Washington."

"Say it another way," she said, barely audible.

"That letter to the New York *Times* I told you to write. You wrote it."

"But I *did* learn," she insisted. "When I began to see how big the problem was I began to think about the answer that was so simple, about everybody stop making them. I mean I began to think of the word *stop* and I thought no matter how you stopped, by yourself or with others, you just had to stop. That's what I thought. And then when we stayed overnight at Cody with those pacifists, they didn't think it was awful to say this country ought to do it alone, they thought it was awful *not* to say it. So I *did* learn," she said, darting an upward glance at him, a begging glance that was more like something of her sister's, and finding no acceptance in his eyes, she lowered her gaze and stuffed a fringed corner of her scarf into her mouth, removing it the next moment in order to speak on. "And I can't help what Emery Fixas did with the letter. It would have been all right to do if *he* hadn't made it seem so terrible."

"Little birds are dining warily and well," he recited

coldly and cruelly, a line from a nonsense rhyme he had read to her, over and over, when she was a child. She had picked up a seed here and a seed there, he thought, remembering her listening figure on the other side of him as he walked with the pacifist youth, and all the little seeds weighed in her craw like wisdom.

Unable to bear his behavior, she again stuffed the fringe into her mouth and retreated down the corridor, weaving a bit from side to side; and his anger against the candidate Fixas and against the situation that her letter had plunged him into was so consuming that it left no room for pity for her.

He returned his gaze to the column of Fixas' speech, found the sentence he had left and read on:

Who is responsible for this man's appointment? The finger points at Harmon Harringer. Let us ask Harringer why this man was appointed. Let us ask still another question. Let us ask him why the cabinet post of Secretary for Humanity was dreamed up in the first place. Did he intend that this figure, this Secretary for Humanity, supply us with promises of peace because he, Harringer, failed to provide for us in the way that it matters? He failed to provide mass shelters until you, the American people, demanded mass shelters. He failed to give his unqualified support to the program for satellite storage and launching of nuclear bombs, preferring not to dare, not to experiment, until the Soviet Union announced it was embarking upon a satellites-for-bombing program. In every aspect of our defense he has failed us, and thus he has failed us in our seeking for peace. The American people demand acts for peace. They demand an increase in the military budget, they demand military satellites, more submarines for nuclear missiles, all of the safeguards they have been deprived of and denied by the present administration. Harmon Harringer knew that he was denying us these necessities for life, and to convince us that he was not denying us, not depriving us, he created his Secretary for Humanity. It was never a reassuring figure. It was, instead, a sign of weakness in this country's defense. A figure that might have triggered a nuclear war and still might trigger it!

Folding up the newspaper, he laid it at one end of the cot and sat down apart from it at the other end, as one sits at a distance from a legal counselor in time of bereavement.

When the lights went out in his cell, leaving him only a dim green light from the corridor, he lay on his cot watching the weird, clustering souls, the little souls, like nightbirds, that rose from the tombs of Egypt, their human faces those of the Wapson *Times* editor (eyes narrowly unwilling to be the victim of another joke), of Radovan, of Eversledge, of Harringer, of Fixas, of Dykes, of the bus driver through Missouri, of Roundup, until they were gone, all flying upward through the ceiling and into the night, and he slept.

At nine in the morning Bernice brought him another Portland paper. It was not crisp, as newly bought newspapers are, and it smelled of menthol, and he knew that it had been read in bed by Alma, anxiously. The headlines were about the photograph that was reproduced right under them, a very large photograph and a bit fuzzy. It was, he saw, a photograph of himself handing something to a woman who was not Alma but standing as close to him as a wife stands. The caption beneath it read: *Woman in Black receives what may prove to be microfilmed U.S. secret documents from Arnold Elkins, Secretary for Humanity. The place: Tokyo International Airport.* The news dispatch from Tokyo explained that a photographer for a Japanese picture magazine, covering the arrival of Nolly Noreen and photographing her from the rear as she sang to the group of soldiers who had come to the airport to welcome her, had noted, upon developing the film, that Secretary Elkins and a woman companion were present among the soldiers in the background. He was able to identify the man in the picture as Elkins, the dispatch read, because he had seen him encircled by citizens in the waiting room later and, inquiring of them, had learned that Elkins was awaiting a plane for the States. On reading of the "Becky Letter" in the Tokyo papers, the photographer had hurried with the print to the U.S. Embassy.

Arnold could not remember ever being in the Tokyo International Airport. The place name, in the context of the dispatch, had the sound of foreign intrigue and the Woman in Black was of a milieu mysterious to him. Then with a shock he identified her: the middle-aged maid of Miss Noreen. He held the paper away from him to enlarge the meaning of the picture as the picture itself had been enlarged, a corner isolated and brought swiftly to the fore.

"I was giving her a cigarette," he said, as much to himself as to Bernice. "She's Miss Noreen's maid or confidante or whatever they call them."

Bernice lifted a finger to point to another item through the bars: *Elkins Whereabouts Unknown.* In that dispatch from Washington, D.C., he read that a spokesman for the Defense Department had told the press that Elkins and his family were on a tour of the nation and that their exact whereabouts was unreported. Arnold sent Bernice to see the deputy at the desk, bearing the newspaper and its photograph as proof of his identity. Assuming that a deputy would return with her to unlock the cell, he was surprised to see her returning alone. They would not release him before noon, she said, and then she left him to return to the hotel.

Within an hour the corridor was filled with footsteps and voices, and from his cot he saw a deputy accompanied by two young men, one of them toting a camera. They were introduced to him as regional reporter and photographer for *Explosion*, and in the midst of this formality, while they were nodding at one another through the bars, the photographer hoisted his camera and clicked the shutter, exploding a flashbulb in his subject's face.

"Every time one of these things goes off," the reporter said in a friendly way, "I am reminded of how excellent a name is *Explosion*. We tend to think too much in terms of long, slow growth or change when, really, explosions occur all the time. Historical ones, such as wars or rebellions; explosions in our personal lives, such as revelations or domestic disasters, births and deaths; and the ones in the scientific field, such as discoveries and inventions, and in the cultural field, the creative explosions in art and literature and music." It was evident to Arnold that the young reporter, knowing that he was an associate professor of history, was chatting to impress him and to gain his respect. "It's dynamic, isn't it?" the young man asked. "That way of looking at things? It helps us to expect the unexpected. Anyway," he smiled, *"Explosion* is always there, covering the big ones and the little ones."

The deputy, with that languidness sometimes affected by persons conscious of their authority, unlocked the door and held it open for the visitors, explaining to Arnold that they had come at the request of the sheriff to check into his contention that he was Arnold Elkins, Secretary for Humanity.

"So they thought you were a traveling salesman, a crooked one?" the reporter asked when the deputy had gone. He sat down on the cot, feeling in his raincoat pockets for his notebook. The photographer sat cross-legged on the floor and with a long reach offered Arnold, on the cot's edge, a cigarette.

"The Wapson *Times* editor misunderstood me," Arnold explained. "He didn't believe me when I told him I was Arnold Elkins, Secretary for Humanity, and he asked me what I was selling. When I told him blueprints for the best kind of shelter, he didn't get the point and accused me of using a cabinet member's name to sell rural shelter plans that are obtainable free from the government."

The young men laughed, and Arnold, confident that, at last, he was talking with rational persons, waited, gratified, until their appreciative laughter ceased, waited for them to inquire of him what he meant by the best kind of shelter, for until that was explained to them they themselves were ignorant of the point.

But his laughter tapering off, the reporter asked, "Did you write the Becky Letter?" And although he asked his question with an intelligent light of inquiry in his eyes, and although it was a necessary question, the one he had been sent to ask, Arnold felt it as a shock to his nervous system, for he had hoped that, with his manner, with his few words, he had impressed them with his natural honesty.

"No," he said. "I did not. If I had written it I would have signed it."

"I suppose it doesn't really matter whether you did or not. Dictated it, I mean," the reporter said. "She got her idea from the gist of your conversations with your family, perhaps?"

"She got it from her own ruminating," he said.

"Is it, as Fixas says, a call for unilateral disarmament? After all," the young man said, reflectively twiddling his pen, "it doesn't say anything about safeguards, about inspection . . ."

"You might try interviewing *her*," Arnold suggested.

"But what do *you* think it means?"

"Usually," he said, "she says what she means. I suppose she said it this time too."

"Well, how do *you* feel about the nuclear weapons problem? You, yourself? Let's forget her and talk about *your* solution," the reporter said, his eagerness escaping through the sibilant last word.

At last, he thought, someone was interviewing him. Not just an editor of a city newspaper but a reporter for the picture magazine with the highest circulation in the country. But the time was out of joint. He was called upon to speak after he had been accused of speaking already—traitorous words with the falsetto voice of a child. All that he would say, that great speech for reason and morality that he had striven to make for the past several weeks, would be only a postscript to the infamous Becky Letter. But, clearing his throat, accepting a light for his cigarette, rubbing his knee hard as flint is rubbed to make it spark, he spoke anyway. Again he denied that he had written the Becky Letter and he offered his own proposal for a conference of all nuclear nations that could not end until, compromise after compromise after compromise, all had relinquished their bombs and their missiles. Then, taking a short, nervous draw on his cigarette, he plunged into the Flugeltaube proposal of total disarmament of all nations concomitant with projects to improve the condition of mankind. As he spoke with desperate articulateness, as the fervency rose in his voice, inside him, like cold creeping through a deep shelter, crept the conviction that whatever he was saying would be used against him, would be fuel for his funeral pyre.

When Arnold had concluded, the reporter slipped his notebook back into his raincoat pocket, and as he was doing this he cocked an eyebrow at Arnold. "Who's the chick in the black dress?" he asked, and when Arnold had told him, he and the photographer laughed together. But again, as with their enjoyment of the traveling salesman story, the real comprehension of his innocence was lacking, for it seemed to Arnold that all through his expounding of his solution they had been under the influence of that front page of the morning papers.

Shaking hands with Arnold, the reporter said, "We can expect Harringer to take up the old cudgel for you. Fixas' smear is directed at *him*, you know. When an appointee accepts a cruise or cashes in on some deal or commits an act of treason, the publicity always reflects on whoever appointed him. We're waiting to see what he does with it."

It cheered him, this possibility that Harringer might defend him because in so doing the President defended himself, and the hope that he might, at last, converse face to face with the man who had no time, no few minutes to grant him, transmitted itself as earnest appreciation to his hand that was shaking the young man's hand.

The rain was still falling, the same drizzling rain that had been falling the hour they arrived in town, when he walked out with Bernice onto the grounds of the county courthouse. The big maple trees were sighing with a surfeit of rain and the green, wet benches under them were strewn with leaves.

"It's raining," Bernice said, wanting him to be conscious of reality, as one points out a relative's face to a victim of shock.

They remained in Wapson, nursing Alma under several thin hotel blankets and a faded pink-cotton bedspread. A gray dishpan of water steamed day and night on the oil stove, moistening the air, and the prescriptions of a local doctor were given her by teaspoon and by capsule.

"She should have written it with lemon juice," Alma said, leaning on her elbow in bed, a capsule in one hand and a glass of water in the other. "So then they would have had to heat it over a match before the writing showed. You know how children send messages? Fixas could have made the most of that. What a document!"

"Take the capsule and lie down," Arnold commanded.

The family drew closer together in that week in Wapson. It was Bernice who got closest to Becky with comfort for she, knowing that her sister had written the letter to counteract her escapade in the shelter, felt responsible herself for that fateful communication. For the first time in the family's history the sisters were sisterly in the fullest sense of the word, one accomplice consoling the other for an act that had proved to be a crime against the family. The rest of the family forgave them, Arnold seeking them out with a contrite face and many small courtesies, and together they all waited for the day when Alma would be well enough for them to leave the town of Wapson for the nation's capital.

Once again during that week he made the headlines of the nation's newspapers, this time with Nolly Noreen, and their pictures were side by side on the front pages. The maid of Miss Noreen, questioned in Hollywood after Arnold had named her as the woman in black, acknowledged this to be true but denied there was anything wrong with being that woman, and her employer, also interviewed, defended her employee's honor and her own as well. It was obvious in her indignant statement to the press that she believed Arnold had attempted to implicate her maid in an act of treason and that he had done this to sully her triumph as Miss Massive Retaliation. The reporters who had come from Portland, Seattle and Salem to see him that first day he had returned to the hotel were given the same long and eloquent reply he had given the *Explosion* reporter, but the excitement of the Nolly Noreen involvement left no room for any answer of his to the world's crisis. Toward the end of the week a heartening item appeared, Harringer's statement at his regular press conference that he would make no comment on Fixas' accusations against Elkins until he spoke with Elkins himself. The Secretary for Humanity, he said, was being summoned back to Washington. The day following this item a telegram from a Presidential secretary arrived at the hotel, instructing Arnold to return by air to the capital. On the morning of the seventh day after his release, Alma being well enough, they boarded a northbound bus to Portland.

From the city's bus depot they rode in a taxi to the Shackleton Plaza Hotel at whose curb the airport bus was stationed. While Alma and the girls waited in the bus Arnold sought the magazine stand in the lobby. The proprietor was stacking even higher an already high pile of *Explosion* among the other lower piles of less popular magazines, and he saw that the cover picture was of himself behind bars. Underneath the picture red letters asked *Who Is Our Secretary for Humanity?* He put a quarter into the proprietor's hand and slipped the top magazine off the pile. Under it the cover was repeated. All down the pile it was repeated, and at every magazine stand in the nation and abroad the high piles were repeated. As he was folding his copy to hide his picture from himself and others, the revolving door and the swinging doors on each side of it were suddenly overburdened by a crowd of men, each wearing a yellow skullcap upon which bobbed, at the top of a short coil, a yellow plastic arrow, a replica of the yellow arrows that he had seen all over the nation pointing to public shelters under construction. They milled through the lobby toward the elevators, and as they passed him he saw pinned to their lapels round identification badges the size of an orange upon which was printed *United Structural Steel Workers Convention* and the name and city of the delegate. Two delegates, clowning through the lobby with their arms around each other, came so close to him that he paused to prevent a collision, and in the moment that they raised their eyes they recognized him.

"Brothers!" one cried. "There's a guy here looks like Benedict Arnold Elkins! Isn't this guy Elkins?" he cried to them all, plaintively.

They came out from the elevators they had just entered, they continued to swarm in through the entrances, and they collected around him and the two men, who remained with their arms around each other as if pitting their brotherness against his malevolent desire to tear the nation asunder.

"Are you Benedict Arnold Elkins?" the vocal one cried.

"I'm Arnold Elkins," he said.

"He admits it, he admits it!" the steelworker cried to the fifty and more of his union brothers. Then, using his companion as a rod to hang onto, he leaned far forward until his nose almost touched Arnold's chin. "You want to admit, while you're admitting, that you're aiming to stop work on all the shelters, bring us all up, the structural steel workers and the carpenters and the cement workers, everybody who's down there working away for their country's defense, stop work and leave the people of this country no place to go? You want to admit that's what you had in mind when you wrote that Becky Letter?"

"Stick with him, baby, and you'll wear chains!" someone shouted, and the crystal chandelier, the heirloom of the establishment, shivered with the laughter of the crowd.

Arnold pushed his way through the conventioneers, surprised that no one laid a hand on him, and then not surprised, for the epithets thrown at him were the equivalent
of stones. Even after he was seated in the airport bus, some
of the crowd from the lobby stood under his window,
shouting at him through the pane.

As the bus coursed through the city to the airport, the
tension eased from his body and he saw that the folded
magazine was twisted in the grip of his fingers. He opened
his hand and slowly the magazine unfolded itself, and
again he saw his face, lugubriously narrow, and the dread
of universal catastrophe that lay in his eyes was converted
by the prison bars into a traitor's fear of his country's wrath.

After turning only a few pages he found a double spread
of photographs of himself and even an old 1920 picture of
his father, looking apprehensive and emaciated at his clut-
tered desk in his small office in Acton, Iowa—an impover-
ished attorney, the caption said, who chose to defend the
indefensible, one among them the murderess, Cora Max-
well, arsenic poisoner of nine boarders. The photographs
of himself were, some of them, so old that he was a stranger
to himself, and all of them were derogatory. They had not
been so, perhaps, at the time they were taken, but they
were now, in the context of dishonor. He gazed at himself
at three years of age, straddling a stuffed donkey in an
amusement park; at himself at seven, squatting on the
ground with a catcher's mitt in his hands, front teeth missing in an unappealing, sourish face; at himself as a junior
in the university, his long legs in shrunken tennis pants,
his arm dangling around the shoulders of an unpretty girl
in tennis shorts, a partner whose name and existence he
had forgotten and whose plain features now robbed him of
taste and popularity. The portrait of himself and family

had been taken late in the evening of the day that news of his appointment had been released by the President's press secretary. In the DeVelbiss *Courier* it had been a photograph of an average family embarrassed by the sudden turning of the public eye; here it was something else. Arnold looked peaked with self-doubting. Alma, beside him, looked her usual lively self but this was unfortunate because her expression, alongside his, implied a simpleminded frivolity; in addition, the mannerism of tipping her head became, when caught by the camera, an adulatory tipping toward her husband reminiscent of a signpost that points with a wooden finger. Bernice, far right, was caught with her lips thinned and her eyes averted toward the margin to avoid the dread future she was convinced lay before them. Becky, far left, had cropped her curls for the coming summer and all that remained, at least for the camera's eye, was a black furlike fringe above her round face, for she had lifted her chin as high as it would go as if she were staring in demented curiosity over a fence. Arnold, gazing at the two pages of pictures, was amazed at how swiftly and thoroughly they had gone about collecting them. Never, he thought, was so much interest shown for the course of a man's life as in the hour of his infamy.

With both hands he twisted the magazine until his hands gave out, and leaning forward he dropped it on the floor under his seat where he could neither see it nor feel it. After a few minutes he put his hand on Alma's knee, and though she was resting with her head back and her eyes closed and had not seen the pictures, he patted her knee reassuringly.

8

On the mahogany dining table in the apartment, under the red glass vase that was empty of the gladioli that the landlady's welcoming hands had so carefully arranged that day of arrival, lay a long white envelope. Arnold, carrying luggage into the bedroom, saw it first and recognized it instantly as an envelope from the President; it was the same heavy, parchmentlike paper as the envelope that had been delivered to him in DeVelbiss a hundred years ago. With clumsy hands he opened it—was it a message requesting him to come at once, the moment he returned to Washington?—and saw that it was a letter of dismissal concisely done in one narrow paragraph that was like a knife wound that he, Elkins, had left in Harringer's trusting back.

The landlady was rapping at the door, an imperious rapping for those persons who have no business in somebody else's apartment. She had heard them go up the stairs and had followed at their heels. Turning the knob from the outside at the same moment that Bernice turned it from the inside, she entered, no longer tremblingly deferential, in a faded yellow housecoat to her shins and quilted plastic house slippers. The sulphur-blond hair was covered with a scarf that tied turban fashion above her eyebrows. So intense was her animosity that her shriveled face was too small to contain the emotion and some of it quivered for release from her poor old cheeks and some of it was conveyed in spittle. "Fast as you can, you get out!" she cried. "You're already packed, there ain't nothing more of yours around. Everything I found on the dressers and in the drawers is in that carton out in the hall." And she flung the door open so that they could see the waist-high cardboard box they had already seen and wondered about.

"No doubt you have read the letter from the President?" Arnold asked, waving it at her.

"What're you accusing me of?" she cried. "It's a penitentiary offense opening messages from the President. Where I got my information from, everybody gets it from. The President was on TV this morning, made what he called a disavowal of you. Said he'd fired you and said a President should not be judged by the conduct of those under him who turned out to be bad, but the thing to do when they were discovered was to get rid of them as fast as possible. So that's what I'm doing, too. Don't sit down here, you don't reside here no more. Give me the key and you and your family go somewhere else."

"My family is tired," Arnold said. "We would like to sleep here for one night."

"The rent ain't paid, anyway!" she informed him. "Nobody paid the rent for September. So out you go!"

She stood at the top of the stairs, her veined old hand grasping her housecoat up against her stomach to prevent her garments being touched by them as, one by one, they descended, Alma first, carrying two suitcases, Bernice, carrying two, Becky, carrying one and his brief case, and Arnold last, his arms embracing the carton, the top of it just under his nose and covered over with newspaper tucked down around the edges. He paused alongside her, kindling a fiery understanding in his eyes, nodding his head encouragingly at the same time. *"Fiat justitia, ruat caelum,"* he said.

"That don't mean nothing to me," she replied defiantly, lowering her eyes.

"It's an old Latin proverb," he explained. "Let justice be done though the heavens fall." And peering around the corner of the carton, he began his descent, feeling her gaze like a prodding broom in his back.

They returned by bus to DeVelbiss. They had rented their modest house to a zoology professor, a woman who was their friend, and returning in the early morning before daylight, they congregated on the front steps and Becky rang the bell, so that the sound of the key in the lock and their footsteps would not panic the woman alone. No one answered the door, no lights went on upstairs, no lights on the porch; and after five minutes in the cold, and after noting that the porch was strewn with rolled-up newspapers, they entered and found that their tenant had fled. She had fled in such haste, in fact, that she had left behind on the kitchen sink a row of jars containing cocoons on twigs, a tree frog, and some small animal's viscera in solution.

Since the name of Arnold Tennyson Elkins was now on the nation's list of the dishonorably discharged, he was excised, also, from the faculty at DeVelbiss College, his leave of absence extended forever, and all the institutions of learning, near and far, to which he applied were prompt with their letters of rejection. While he wrote and waited and was, every day, rejected, he took up again for half a day his "Cultural History of Iowa" for the *DeVelbiss College Quarterly* until he realized that, despite its value, it would not be acceptable to the editors.

On the eve of election day, they saw on their television set political commentators and analysts predict the defeat of Harringer, and one of the reasons for that defeat, they said, was his creation of the cabinet post of Secretary for Humanity; and when he was, indeed, defeated at the polls that reason seemed sound enough. A few days after the election, James Eversledge, Secretary of Defense, in a televised public address at a brand-new chemical plant in Tennessee embarking upon the production of chemical warfare agents, criticized Harmon Harringer for saddling him with a completely superfluous Secretary for Humanity. A few days following that address, the headlines of the De-Velbiss *Courier* told of Emery Fixas' intention to retain Eversledge as his Defense Secretary, and the item below the headlines quoted Fixas to the effect that Eversledge would henceforth conduct the defense of the nation unhampered and unshackled by the whims and fancies of men less capable than he. A few days before Inauguration Day, Harmon Harringer was aided in the recovery of his self-esteem by his appointment to the chief administrative post of a great university, and within the month the local paper carried a newsworthy photograph of the ex-President strolling, smiling, under the elms of the campus with a crew-cut, crepe-soled student at his side. But Arnold T.

Elkins remained defeated. Although charges against him were never substantiated and a few columnists who supported the party of Harringer devoted some space to reminding their readers of this lack of evidence, accusing Fixas of making political hay of a letter written in complete naïveté by a thirteen-year-old girl, still, with Harringer's dismissal of him over the television networks, a last gate had been closed with a loud clang between Elkins and society. Late in February a small box arrived from Washington, D.C., and within it he found the few possessions he had left on his desk in the Triangle, the lion and the pen and the calendar, along with a shoehorn that was not his.

In the spring of the year, after a winter that was as barren of good tidings as the earth was hard, the Elkins family left the town of DeVelbiss, enabled by the down payment from the sale of their house and furnishings to pay their train fare to Chicago, rent an apartment there, and eat three meals a day while Arnold and his wife looked for work, taking the names of Lucille and Willard Malloy.

It was to the advantage of the Elkins family in its pursuit of sustenance that the physical appearance of the parents had changed considerably that winter. Arnold was gaunt and his hair gray. Alma's face had become somewhat bony, and in order to appear younger she touched up the gray in her hair with a dead-black dye, a practice that helped to devitalize her once lively looks. The girls, also, had changed. Bernice, finding that she was able to survive the family's own peculiar calamity was now no longer disabled by her fear of the much larger calamity, and to give herself the visage, among her schoolmates, of one who has the courage of her convictions, she declared herself a party to the Becky Letter, claiming that she and her sister had written it together. And that classic brow of hers which often, to Arnold, had shown the unoriginal, somewhat vacuous cast that such brows sometimes show, was now the sign of sobriety that it is often mistaken for.

One afternoon, shortly after they had moved to Chicago, Arnold, coming upon Becky asleep on the sofa, was surprised to see that her face no longer glowed in sleep. Then remembering that he had known this fact for some years and that the phenomenon belonged to early childhood, he realized that the change he saw was another, more recent change. The child's clues to what kind of woman she would become were no longer clues but part and parcel of the young woman herself.

At the Giant $ Store, Alma was hired as a clerk and assigned to the toy department. She did well enough with dolls and Tinker Toys, but her reluctance to demonstrate the miniature missiles, all set up on opposing sides of a large piece of plywood painted with oceans and continents and controlled by a dozen push buttons, aroused the curiosity of the manager of the department, and after only three weeks she was discharged. The personnel counselor to whom she had been sent had attempted to draw from her what he called the unconscious reason for her antipathy toward that particular toy. He was a young man, plump, fair, curly-haired, and his framed doctorate in psychology hung on the wall behind him. She informed him that her reason was a conscious one, that she feared war and weapons of destruction; and the day following, dismissed at closing time by the department manager, she read, from where she sat across the desk from him, the note that the counselor had penciled on a yellow card. It read, upside down to her: *paranoid delusions of persecution.*

The jobs that Arnold found as Willard Malloy were always terminated by knowledge of his true identity. Someone recognized him, or jobs listed on employment

applications as previously held were found, on routine veri-
fication, to be false. The job of longest duration was as a
pot scrubber in the county hospital. Down in that basement
kitchen, in the clatter and steam and mingled strong odors,
his identity was lost, he became another anonymous pot
washer, this one thin and taciturn, in a long procession of
pot washers hired from the street and the culinary union,
and impermanent as parings. But after six weeks, the last
day came. A total of four busboys failed to report for work
that day, and the kitchen supervisor tossed Arnold a clean
white apron and told him to get breakfast to the patients.
So Arnold wiped his hands, removed his damp, grayish
apron, donned the clean one, pushed the steel food cart
into the elevator, rode up with it to its assigned ward, and
descended for another cart.

In that huge beehive of wards, he was pleased that he
met no interest in himself as a person. Those who were
too sick to eat saw nothing, and those who were well
enough to be hungry saw only the food or were engaged in
adjusting their beds to a comfortable slant for mealtime.
But in the men's cardiac ward, where patients in gray paja-
mas sat propped by pillows in the narrow beds or sat in
bedside chairs, at the moment when the nurse took the
cart from him and began to serve the patients, a haggard,
bespectacled man with the pearly skin of the institution-
alized and the dying, drew himself erect and, shaking his
fist at Arnold, cried, "It's him! It's Elkins! Surround him!
There's a Russian sub in the lake! If he gets away, that's
where he's headed. Surround him, I say!" Then clasping
his chest, he collapsed, and two other nurses who had come
to the door in response to his shouting, ran to administer
to him.

A few minutes before noon, the chief administrator himself came down into the kitchen to dismiss Arnold from

hospital employment. Arnold saw that the handsome, heavy man in the dark expensive suit was a bit shaky with the excitement of this encounter with the notorious Arnold T. Elkins, who had sunk from the cabinet of the President of the United States to the basement of this county hospital, and who stood, depleted, in a dishwasher's apron, wiping with his sleeve the rivulets of sweat on his face. The only words the administrator was able to say were, "That man died up there," but those few words elevated the victim of the heart attack to a symbolic level. He became the entire nation which, if Arnold's advice in the Becky Letter had been acted upon, would have died cataclysmically. Arnold untied his apron, shrugged on his overcoat, and went out into the streets.

In the middle of summer, over a year from the day he had received the letter from President Harringer offering him the cabinet post, Arnold, fired the day before from a janitor-gardener job in a private sanitarium, after the superintendent had struck up a conversation in the rose garden to verify his suspicions, found himself one afternoon gazing through the aperture of a fence surrounding a mass shelter site. He was sick of bending over sinks in the steamy, malodorous air of restaurant kitchens, sick of jobs in cell-like elevators in old loft buildings, and most of all he was sick of laboring alone. He had avoided as long as he could the descent into the shelters, but now the mass shelter that opened below him, its concrete floor and its scaffolded sides swarming with the tiny figures of workers in yellow helmets, drew him down like the depths of his own despair.

He entered the yellow shack alongside the fence. The superintendent, a lean fellow with a tan cotton hat, a tan shirt, and heavy-soled shoes that laced halfway up his calves, was leaning over a desk laden with blueprints and tracing paper. A blue-and-red tattoo of a missile covered the back of his right hand gripping the desk's edge. Without straightening up or taking his eyes from the blueprints, he asked Arnold if he was experienced in concrete construction and Arnold replied that he had worked on shelters across the country. The superintendent then instructed him to see the timekeeper at the other door of the partitioned shack and, as Arnold turned to go, the man glanced over his shoulder at him. "You been in bed?" he asked.

"Not since this morning," Arnold replied.

"You look like you ain't been up and around," the superintendent explained, his narrow mouth smiling a concern in which the rest of the man did not participate.

The stout, blue-shirted timekeeper leaned on the lower half of his door and scribbled on a pink slip. Behind him were piles of yellow helmets and tools and equipment marked with yellow paint. "Midnight shift," he said.

"Is that something new?" Arnold asked, remembering that when he had left the restaurant kitchens in the hours after midnight the shelter excavations had been silent and dark along the route of the homeward bus.

"We're rushing it now," the timekeeper explained. "Fixas ordered it last night because of what that Russian general said yesterday, that our shelter program means we're aiming to start a war, get our people underground and send the missiles over. Fixas says they're using it as their excuse to attack *us*. The first one over in this kind of a war has the advantage, you know. He says they may attack us before we attack them even if we aren't aiming to attack them. They're saying we're aiming to do it and we're saying they're aiming to do it. Anyway, we're rushing the shelters all over the country. You can expect to get rushed yourself."

Another applicant from off the street, a man of fifty in a faded orange shirt, caught up with Arnold as he left the shack and together they walked to the laborers' union hall to join. "The thing I'm afraid of," he said, walking with an urgent companionability, "is what do we do for air?" The skin of his lips was a slick gray from the heat of the day.

"Air?" asked Arnold.

"When the bombs start hitting," the man explained. "We may have to stay down a long time. I'm not talking about ground zero, about never coming up. I'm talking about just having to stay down. What do we do for air?"

"The shelters are air-conditioned," Arnold said.

"But what do you do if the air that's coming in has the stuff in it?" the man persisted.

"I suppose they close off the system," Arnold ventured.

"That's what I mean," the man said, his walk jolting his voice up and down as if it had broken loose from a mooring in his throat. "Where's the air coming from then?"

"Maybe they'll pipe in oxygen from underground deposits, as they do natural gas. The best minds are at work on the problem, no doubt," Arnold said.

"But what if the pipes get broke in the blast? Where's the air coming from then?"

"Air," said Arnold, "is a minor item when everything else is also missing." He saw that his companion received this comment with the lapsed look of one wondering whether to be relieved or stricken.

With ninety other laborers he waited under floodlights at midnight. As he stood among the shifting men by the hiring shack, all donning yellow helmets and pinning on their numbered plastic badges, he recalled that day a year ago when he had spent an hour in the park across from the campus watching the machines begin the excavation for the DeVelbiss public shelter. Since that day he had seen more shelters in various stages of construction and always he had tasted concrete dust thick on his tongue—the dust of demolished sidewalks or of the mixture recently dried. As he was herded now with the other laborers onto a huge lift, he tasted the dust again and it was, he felt, the dust of the end, and it had begun to fall that first day when the first jackhammers began to jump.

The walls rose around him as the lift sank halfway down, and there at the level of the scaffolding the men shuffled off onto a platform upon which stood rows of concrete buggies like two-wheeled metal baby buggies encrusted with hard, gray frilling. The laborers' foreman told them to load the buggies under the hopper that hung in the air over the platform, a huge metal funnel, oily from its lift cables. Arnold stood in line with his buggy, and when it was weighed down with the concrete pouring into it, he followed the other laborers along the runway of the scaffolding to a far corner where several laborers were stirring the concrete that the rest were dumping in. The pit was filled with the sounds of persevering chaos, the whirr of the vibrators that were like long snakes in the laborers' hands, their captive energy agitating the concrete down in the wooden forms. Arnold tilted his buggy forward, saw his load spill over and mix with the rest that was rising around the steel rods, then he continued on along the runway, following the others around the sides of the deep, square pit. As he hustled along, his yellow helmet making his head feel odd, the handles of the buggy jolting his arms, he glanced up in hope of finding the night sky and its stars, but his eyes were seared by the intense stare of the floodlights above the pit.

Quickly he lowered his head, and when his sight returned to him he saw that he was again in line for the hopper and when his buggy was filled he pushed it again along the scaffolding.